ADAM C. FRANCE

The World Hovering Around Me

This novel is entirely a work of fiction. The names, characters and incidents portrayed in it are the work of the author's imagination. Any resemblance to actual persons, living or dead, events or localities is entirely coincidental.

Adam C. France asserts the moral right to be identified as the author of this work.

First edition

ISBN: 979-8-9907312-2-6

This book was professionally typeset on Reedsy.
Find out more at reedsy.com

Chapter One

It was six o'clock in the morning. The only way I knew this was the faint sun peeking through the openings between the buildings and the thud of the newspapers as they were thrown from the van on the road outside my tent, each landing at the door of the businesses that lined the sidewalk. In the short three weeks I had called this my home, the sounds of the streets became my wake-up call. Otherwise, I wouldn't have known the time of day, as my life had become one long trudge through minutes, hours, and days—from tent to dumpster, from dumpster to soup kitchen, from soup kitchen to... to whatever came next.

Sometimes I would find myself walking along the pier aimlessly, hiding my face from the crowds of people filing in and out of shops and restaurants. Other times I would find myself sitting in the corner of an alleyway, hiding behind heaps of garbage. My days were spent either in search of or hiding from—in search of my next meal or a warm jacket, or a place to sleep—hiding from hunger, from sight, from a life I was ashamed to be living.

It was six o'clock in the morning and I wished I had reason to rise, at least more reason than to relieve the pain in my stomach. The last meal I had was maybe forty-eight hours ago. If you can even call it a meal—a few scraps from a dumpster behind a pizza place near where I normally slept. Since then I had felt nauseous and I am sure I had a fever, as I woke up hot and sweaty on a forty-degree morning.

I lay there, thoughts of a life that seemed so far away invaded my subconscious. A warm bed. Roommates bustling around the room, readying themselves for their morning classes. Still an hour before I had to leave for my nine a.m. class. I was comfortable and safe in my middle-class bubble.

The door opened. The door closed. I was alone in my own comfort, blanket pulled up to my chin. Eyes closed. A feeling of contentment flowed through my body. I drifted off, catching the last bit of sleep I could before rising and filling my stomach with food from a dorm-sized fridge at the side of my bed.

Soon my alarm sounded. I reached over and gently patted the top of my alarm clock, silencing the intermittent buzz-buzz, buzz-buzz. I sat up and allowed myself time to waken to the new day. I was a bit tired from two nights of cramming for midterms, the first of which was in just forty minutes—an exam for which I felt fully prepared.

I swung my feet over the edge of the bed, reached for the ceiling, and yawned. I stood slowly and then knelt on the ground in front of my fridge and pawed through its contents. A small apple juice, a yogurt, and a half-eaten bagel. I didn't think twice. I just filled my belly.

A few minutes later I was rifling through my closet to find my left shoe. For some reason, I always seemed to set each shoe in opposite corners of the room as I came home for the night and haphazardly made myself comfortable. Then, when needed the next morning, I could only find one. I exited my closet and did a three-sixty, scanning the room for the displaced object, my eyes finally landing on what could only be the toe of my shoe peeking out from under my bed.

I limped over to the bed, sock and shoe on my right foot, sock only on my left. This, in my middle-class bubble, was the biggest obstacle I would face—a misplaced shoe. I leaned down, pulled out the missing article, and slid it on my foot. Problem solved.

Today's problem, though, on that forty-degree morning, was where to now. The soup kitchen was a mile away, but good scraps could be found behind the many restaurants in a four-block radius. The dilemma—chance the rancid garbage and inevitable stomach-churning or walk the mile and wait in the two-block line for runny eggs and stale bacon. How I longed for the half-eaten bagel in my dorm room fridge... even with the missing shoe.

I unzipped my tent and peered out the door. The sidewalk was beginning to fill with people, coffee in hand, hustling to one of the offices high above the street, many with a view of the fish market and the glistening waters below. I turned back inside my tent and began my morning ritual—rolling up my sleeping bag, stuffing my few belongings into my backpack, and then taking my tent down and storing it away in its long-faded blue sack. These tasks became a necessity early on when I learned the hard way that nothing's safe on the streets once it was out of arm's reach.

I brushed my teeth with a toothbrush I kept in my pocket, using salt from packets I swiped from McDonald's a few days earlier as makeshift toothpaste. I rinsed my mouth with the last of the restroom water I had in an old Avion bottle, spit in a small garbage can near my sidewalk home, and set out on the mile-long trudge to breakfast, backpack securely on my back, full of my life's possessions, my portable home carried under my arm.

I was now pretty familiar with my surroundings, though I still made rookie mistakes, one of which was forgetting that not only was I living on the streets, I looked and smelled like I was living on the streets. Catching a glimpse of myself in a store window was all I needed to jar myself back to reality, a reality I tried to push out of my mind each and every day. Much of the time I still thought of myself as the person I was, just a few short months ago—a successful college student in my first year of undergrad. Yet, in reality, a whirlwind of unforeseen circumstances brought that life to an abrupt end.

It was not long after midterms of spring semester my freshman year. I received notice that my student loans were denied and I owed a full semester of tuition to be paid by month's end or I would be dropped from all my classes and would have to vacate my dorm room.

After a stress-filled two weeks of frantic phone calls, emails, and trips to the financial aid office, I figured it out. I didn't solve the problem, but I did solve the mystery. My parents did not fill out their portion of the FAFSA and I would not be eligible for student loans until they did so, which wouldn't be in time to cover the current twelve-thousand dollars for my spring dorm and class bill. I was shocked. I knew they didn't take the news well when I told them, but I never thought they would abandon me, not fill out the paperwork, leaving me high and dry without warning. Our last interaction was not pleasant, but right before we sat down and I told them, we had gone over my FAFSA application and they planned on finishing it the following day. But sadly, it did make sense. My uptight, bible-thumping parents, who had me and my siblings pray before

4

each meal and read bible verses before bed, were shocked when I told them I was gay.

"No you're not," my mom replied in haste. "You were the captain of the football team. You had girlfriends in high school."

My dad just sat there, turned away from me, and said nothing.

A few weeks later, I had my answer. I knew my parents had turned their back on me.

I called. My mom reluctantly answered. I told her my situation. I told her I had nowhere to go and would need to come home until this was worked out.

I sat on a silent phone. She didn't say a word.

Finally, she broke the silence. "You're not welcome here until you come to your senses."

"Mom?" I questioned. "What do you mean?"

"You need to figure this out yourself."

"Can I talk to dad?"

"Your dad doesn't want to speak with you."

And that was it. The line went dead.

Come to my senses? I asked myself. *Figure this out?* The only thing to figure out is why my parents were abandoning their eldest child—the child they drove all around the state and up and down the West Coast, sitting in bleachers every weekend during football and baseball season through middle and high school.

Most of my friends were in college or the military, but I was still able to find couches to sleep on the next two months. I stayed with one of my friend's parents for two weeks, but could tell I overstayed my welcome—I'm sure my parents had something to do with that. Then I split time on the couches of the only two friends still in the area, one drank too much and

5

his apartment smelled like weed all the time. The other was struggling to make rent, so I got a job, but by the time I got my first measly paycheck he had lost his job and we couldn't make ends meet. Now I made my way to the soup kitchen—strangely enough though, it had become a place of solace. While it wasn't my idea of fine dining, I felt accepted and seen there. No judgments. And now that I had no home, no friends' couches to sleep on, I had to take what I could get.

There was a rotating group of pastors who shared meals with us. They never preached, formally or informally. They just talked and took an interest. I noticed that one pastor, in particular, seemed to really understand life on the streets. He was usually there two or three mornings a week. He is one reason I was willing to wait in line for the stale bacon.

After visiting the mission a few times, I made it a point to find ways to talk with Pastor Jim, the pastor who so easily sat next to dirty homeless people and blended into the conversation. He had a way of connecting with everyone that made each individual feel important and made it easy to open up. One morning, I was telling him how I had only been on the street for a short while. I didn't go into great detail, but did tell him I had a falling out with my parents. He looked at me, softly put his hand on my shoulder, and told me he was homeless when he was young as well. He said he was saved by the church and then eventually he dedicated his life to God. This was the first time he had really brought up religion, but the way he presented it felt natural. He was not pushing it on me. He was being genuine. He was opening himself up to me, treating me like a normal human being. He just shared his story as I had shared mine. I was always used to religion being forced upon me—this is the way you pray, this is what you need to believe.

6

While my time at the soup kitchen was nice, I didn't make it there every day, or more precisely, very often. Depending on where I pitched my tent and how I felt when I woke up, I may lay in bed, hoping to sleep through my empty stomach while the street woke up and the throngs of people buzzed around. Many mornings it felt as if the world was hovering around me—life was going on, people were going about their lives while I huddled up in my tent, invisible. But on this forty-degree morning, I made my way to my first meal in two days, anticipating a cold wait in a long line.

Still a few blocks away, I looked forward and saw the last man standing. The line was at least two blocks long. I picked up my gait and hurried to find my spot at the end knowing that if I was too far back, there would be slim-pickens once I made it inside.

It was amazing how out of place I felt just a few weeks ago, but how at home I felt in that line now. I still remember how reluctant I was, just three days into my life on the street. The smell alone made me gag. But now I noticed nothing, it was a part of the life I was living, no matter how far out of my mind I tried to push my reality.

I kept my gaze toward the ground. One thing I learned quickly is not to interact with those you don't know. Don't look people in the eye, you never know how they are going to react. Some street people were very open and were looking for conversation, but, unless you knew them personally, you never knew who those people were, and staring down the wrong person could be costly.

I stood there silently, keeping to myself as the line slowly crept forward. I had not lived on the street long enough to gain friends or create a rep, good or bad. I had to put in the time. I had to stay patient. But, I was sure I wouldn't be on the street long enough for it to matter. I didn't know how I was going to right the ship, but my denial was strong enough to know that it wouldn't be long. Whatever that means. So, my silence would be short-lived, I thought to myself. And that was all I needed to tell myself to give me a small slice of hope.

As the sun began to warm the air, I made it to the front of the line, checked in, and grabbed my food tray. I walked inside. My hands began to tingle as the warm air enveloped my fingers. I slowly scanned the cafeteria as I made my way to the food line. Tables were filled with people—filthy people—young and old, men and women. And I would soon be joining and blending in with the nameless masses who, for a short meal, found respite from the streets.

I walked and nodded at each of the servers who pleasantly smiled and scooped food onto my tray, then turned and again scanned the tables of people, this time, looking for an open seat. I spotted a half-filled table in the middle of the room and found my way over, set my backpack and tent on the ground, and sat down.

While I scooped spoonfuls of scrambled eggs into my mouth, I found myself hoping that Pastor Jim was sitting at one of the nearby tables. Our last conversation had been cut short as a ruckus arose across the room and he was called to assist. He had just revealed his early life on the streets before he accepted Jesus into his life. I was drawn toward his ability to share with and relate to street life without preaching, without pushing an agenda. I wanted to hear more and I wanted to share parts of my life with him.

I picked up a burnt piece of bacon and heard the crunch deep between my ears as I chewed, remembering the crispy ends of bacon my mom used to cut off and put on the edge of the serving plate that she set on the dining room table each Sunday morning. As we ate, she would remind us that this meal, "Nourishes and prepares our hearts and minds for a morning worshiping God." I drifted into a short reverie and found myself floating in memory of a life that once was—a morning breakfast with mom, dad, and siblings, dressed in our Sunday's best. My thoughts moved quickly from warmth and love, a slight smile on my face, to judgment and frustration, smile evaporating. I now looked at my elders as hypocrites and myself as naive. I longed for my life that lived in the past, that existed in my earlier naivete, yet embraced my newfound knowledge. I lived a life of destitution, yet I was liberated by new thoughts and emotions.

I floated back to reality and then turned my head to each side, hoping to find a familiar face, hoping that familiar face was Pastor Jim. I finally spotted him and a few patrons of the soup kitchen standing in the far corner sharing conversation. I cocked my head and watched as they talked. It was a conversation among men. It was a conversation of respect. It was not the homeless and the church, but human beings in discourse, talking politics or education, or family. They could be at a summer BBQ in the backyard of a friend's house laughing about the day's events or at a local bar sharing stories over a cold beer.

I stood up and cleared my table, dumping my garbage and returning my tray. I stood for a moment, thinking of a way to join the conversation in the corner. I turned and peered over. The conversation had slowed, the group was disbanding. Pastor Jim was walking toward the front of the room.

I moved in his direction, trying to make our chance meeting look just like that—chance. I was nervous. I was ashamed of my circumstances. My confidence shrank as I approached him. I took a deep breath and cleared my throat, "Hey, Pastor," I stammered as our paths intersected.

"Hey—how are you doing today?"

"As well as can be expected," I replied, trying to sound as cheerful as possible—trying to hide everything that was stamped as clear as day on my face, my dirty clothes, my messy hair. I looked down at my feet and stuttered, "Not sure if you remember, umm... but we met last week."

"Yes—I remember. You told me about your experience in college."

"Right." I looked up with surprise. His reply filled me with a half confidence. "Well, I've been thinking about a couple things you said."

"And what might that be?" he asked, a genuine look of interest on his face.

"Well—you used to be homeless."

"Yes—many years ago."

"And you found a way out."

"Yeah—it was a tough road, but well worth it."

"I'm sure it was." I paused to muster up a bit more confidence. "And I've been thinking about what you said since last week." I raised my eyes and finally looked at him with determination. "I need to find my way out."

"Good." He nodded and smiled. "That's the first step. Making it a need. Not a want or a desire, but a need."

I looked down again. "I have a couple questions." I closed my eyes and took a soft breath in and out. "I mean—I need to share something with you first."

"Of course. Go right ahead."

I stopped for a moment. What was once background noise,

the clanking of silverware—the murmuring conversations that filled the room—seemed to break my concentration. I looked around.

"Don't worry. Whatever you have to share will stay with me."

I cleared my throat. "Hmmm—umm—I wasn't totally open with you about why I left school."

"Okay?" He nodded, a caring look of interest in his eyes.

"My parents abandoned me and I lost my financial aid because they didn't complete the paperwork. And when I was kicked out of my dorm, they didn't allow me back in the house."

"Can I ask why they did that?"

"Uhhh—yeah. My parents are very religious. We attended church every Sunday and sometimes on Wednesdays. We said prayers before meals every day and did volunteer service through our church. Most of our family time was wrapped around church events." I paused for a moment. "Last spring I finally found the guts to tell them I'm gay." Suddenly my heart felt like it was beating out of my chest. I took a quick breath. "It took a lot for me to be open with them."

"I'm sure it did."

"I knew they weren't going to like it, but I never realized they would disown me." A lump began to form in my gut. I could feel a well of emotions clouding my thoughts. I shook my head. "They were supposed to fill out some paperwork for my student loans the next day, but didn't, and never told me. I didn't know anything was wrong until I got an email about my tuition and dorm fees. And then a few weeks later I was removed from my classes and kicked out of residency.'

"Oh, I'm sorry." He pursed his lips, brows furrowed.

"And my parents wouldn't let me stay with them anymore. In fact, my dad wouldn't even talk to me."

"Wow." He shook his head gently.

"I stayed at friends' houses for a while, but that fell apart quickly. And then without knowing it—I eventually ended up on the street."

He reached out and softly touched my hand. "Thanks for sharing. I'm glad you're able to open up about it and I'm glad you've made the choice to find your way out of this situation."

"Yeah—thank you, Pastor ."

"For me, it took just one thing to get myself moving in the right direction," he said. " I decided that getting off the street was as important to me as my next meal. If I would spend hours scrounging food for dinner, I would spend twice as much time figuring out how to get my life back on track."

"Oh, yeah. I'll do the work."

"Like I said, it wasn't easy. It was one decision, but also lots of hard work."

"As long as there's a way out, I'm willing to work for it."

"Okay, well, first off, I want you to go to Christopher House." He pulled out a card, flipped it over, and wrote down the name and address. "It's an LGBTQ-friendly mission that deals with people on the streets. They can find you clean clothes and provide meals. They also have a computer room that people can use in exchange for volunteer service—usually, light cleaning and maybe serving meals. Talk with Jeremiah Bailey. He's in charge of outreach and can help connect you with homeless resources for college students and he may be able to find you some temporary shelter to get you off the street for a while." He handed me the card.

"Man, that's amazing. Thanks." I stared at the gray rectangular lifeline.

"Flip it over. That's my contact info and the address of my

church. I want to see you there this Sunday." He smiled and winked. "No obligation. I just want to touch base with you and make sure you made a connection."

"For sure. I'll be there." I pocketed the card, looked at him, and smiled back.

"Okay then. Stay safe."

"I will. Thanks, Pastor ." I stood and watched as he turned and made his way to a group of people milling around a table in the far corner. Then, I patted my pocket and nodded my head. Not only was my belly finally full, but my mind was full of hope, and my body full of newfound energy.

I exited the building into the sunny crisp morning air. A breeze brushed across my face. I squinted, took a deep breath, and started walking back toward my usual resting spot, the street corner I had called home for the past twenty-one days. But after a few paces, I stopped.

I inserted my hand into my right pocket and pulled out the card. I read the address of the church and calculated the distance in my head—*maybe two miles.* I turned the card over and read the address for Christopher House. *A mile in the opposite direction,* I said to myself.

I found a seat on a bench on the side of the road, set my backpack and tent beside me, and focused my mind. I had to make a plan. I didn't want to run to one side of town and then have to trek to the other every day. I shuffled through ideas in my head until they started to come together.

I quietly talked through my plan. "I will find my way to Christopher House, spend the next two days figuring things out there, and then camp out near the church on Saturday night." I sat a little longer, closed my eyes, and let the cool air flow over my body, my thoughts solidifying and becoming more clear.

A few minutes later I stood up and gathered my belongings. I turned and headed to the curb, pushing the button on the pole and waiting for the signal to beckon me across when I realized what I had just done. I was the homeless man on the bench talking to himself. I grimaced as the image jolted me back to reality. The light changed and the red flashing hand switched to a white figure in the act of walking. I stepped off the corner and, as I walked across the intersection, vowed that that image, the image of the crazy homeless man speaking gibberish to no one, is not who I am. *I will find my way back,* I thought to myself.

Chapter Two

The building was nestled among the businesses and restaurants a block off the main thoroughfare. A few people huddled by tents and makeshift beds in front of the entrance. People passed by with no nod of acknowledgment to Christopher House or the homeless masses displayed outside its doors. It had all become a part of the normalcy of life in the city.

The sign above the door looked to be recently painted—big white letters, outlined in black, over a rainbow of mismatched colors. I hesitated and looked around, clutching my home under my right arm and feeling the weight of my life's belongings on my back. I looked at the large windows on either side of the door and examined the multitude of fliers that blocked the view inside—church services, jobs, clothes, BLM rallies, concerts, free medical exams, LGBTQIA+ support groups.

I approached the door and reached for the worn brass handle, pressing the latch at the top with my thumb, slowly pulling it open and revealing a small waiting room containing a warn brown wooden desk with a monitor and phone sitting atop, three blue plastic chairs along the opposite wall, and a coffee table scattered with pamphlets and a bowl of condoms with a sign that read, *Take One and Be Safe.* The only thing covering the dirty, white walls was a pride flag above a door adjacent to the entrance and a flier just to the left of the door advertising an upcoming *Celebration of Differences.*

Not knowing what to do, I sat on one of the blue plastic chairs, and waited, thinking someone must be charged with greeting patrons. I picked up a flier from the coffee table and read: *High School Completion/GED.* I set it down and picked up another, *Christopher House Sunrise Service, Wednesdays at 7:00 a.m.* I rifled through the remaining fliers until I came across one that caught my eye—*College, the way off the street.*

The door under the pride flag opened and an elderly woman walked into the room. I stood up, stuffed the flier into my backpack, and looked her way. She walked hurriedly to the desk, followed by two men in dirty coveralls, and reached into one of the desk drawers, "Ahh, here's the number." She turned and presented a piece of paper to one of the men. "Give him a call and he will tell you where to deliver the food."

"Thanks, Nadine," the worker replied. "We'll come back tomorrow with the last few boxes of clothes."

"Sounds Good Jimmy. See you tomorrow." As the workers left, she quickly turned her attention to me. "Hello, young man. Sorry to keep you waiting. What can I do for you?"

"Well, is a—is Jeremiah Bailey here?"

"He won't be back until just before dinner. What exactly do you need?"

"Pastor Jim gave me his name. Said he may be able to help."

"I'm sure he can. He has quite the connections. But, despite the look of it, I do much of the leg work around here." She winked and chuckled softly and it took me just about twenty-four hours to find out she wasn't joking. She was the motor that kept things going and I was fortunate she walked through the door.

"What are you looking for? I'm sure I can get the ball rolling," she said with a smile.

And that's exactly what happened. Less than fifteen minutes later, I had a locker in the back room where I secured my belongings, and was in a hot shower watching a few weeks' worth of dirt flow down the drain. When I emerged from the water, clean clothes, a toothbrush and toothpaste, and deodorant lay beside a towel on a bench. And, a plaid shirt, jeans, and appropriate undergarments hung on pegs on the wall.

I took my time dressing—it had been a long time since I felt clean and was able to relax as I dressed like a normal human being—and then I found myself sitting at a table outside the shower room, devouring a ham sandwich and bottled water. Nadine had not asked me who I was. She had not questioned my motives. She just asked me what I needed and went into action. I gave her a few sparse details and she filled in the blanks.

Over the next few weeks, I had a bed, along with about a dozen other men in similar situations, in a dormitory at the back of the building. We shared in odd jobs—serving meals, eating ours either before or after we were done, sorting through donated clothes, and handing out food to other homeless people on the streets. I started to feel good about myself again. The connection to Christopher House—the daily work, keeping busy—gave me a sense of purpose.

That first night, after I polished off my ham sandwich, I met Jeremiah Bailey. I introduced myself, pulled from my bag that last flier that caught my eye—*College, the way off the street*—and handed it to him. I explained how my parents threw me out when I told them I was gay, and that I was determined to get back into college. Over the next couple of months, with help

17

from both Nadine and Jeremiah, I filled out my FAFSA and re-enrollment paperwork in the makeshift computer room at the back, using Christopher House as my home address. I was now living in a group home for men a mile away, but got up early every morning and walked that mile to Christopher House, rain or shine, to help set up and serve breakfast, and do whatever work needed doing.

At the beginning of the next calendar year, just a week after New Year's and nine months after losing my spot in the dorms and being removed from my classes, I received two emails that changed my life. First, an email from college admissions. I was accepted for late enrollment into spring semester. Second, my student loans would be dispersed to my college account on the first of the month.

I sat in the small room, dimly lit by the flickering fluorescent lighting above, heart pounding, staring at the screen. I scrolled further down my inbox and another email caught my eye. The tagline: *Campus Housing.* I clicked, waited for the message to load, and quickly read four sentences that solidified it all. *You have been approved for spring housing. You have been assigned to Junction House room 143. Reply by January 8 for acceptance. Move-in day is January 28, 8:00 a.m. to 2:00 p.m. You will receive further information in a confirmation email.*

I sat in disbelief looking at a blue highlighted link. All I needed to do was click and accept my new temporary home. I took a breath, clicked, and envisioned myself lying snug in my new bed, next to my dorm-sized fridge, food within arm's reach.

Less than a week later, I had confirmation of my classes, three entry-level undergrad courses to get me going, and an email from my resident advisor welcoming me to a new term. I spent the next two weeks gathering the bare necessities I would need to furnish my dorm room and start my classes while I waited for my student loans to post to my account. Fortunately, I signed up for a meal plan, so I could count on three squares a day. But, I didn't have a working laptop—the one I carried in my backpack had been through quite a lot on my beat around town—and I would have to make do without one until my loans came through.

Chapter Three

The clicking of the keyboards in the corner of the library became a recurring sound in my daily routine. Sometimes I was the only one plucking away in the late hours before closing. Other times, a symphony of click-clicks reverberated off the walls and danced around the air above the cubicles.

It was halfway through spring quarter—just over a year since my premature departure from school. I hadn't really had time to think about it, but for some reason, as I sat, struggling to finish my first term paper, my mind shifted. I pushed my chair back from the computer, looked up at the ceiling, and closed my eyes. I took a deep breath as images and sounds of my struggle drifted through my head—nights in a cold tent, sirens blaring as they drove past my makeshift home—packing boxes of food onto trucks at Christopher House—handing sack lunches and warm socks to other homeless persons on the street.

I opened my eyes and looked at the screen in front of me. I read the title of my paper, "The Invisible Masses: Walking Passed Humanity." My first effort to tell my story and talk about my experiences. It was for my Intro to Sociology class. The assignment was to pick an experience in my life that demonstrated the relationship between individual and community. My thesis: individuals helping individuals make the community whole. Conversely, I made the argument that most people believe organizations, government, and big movements make the community. I was set to use my experience of homelessness to prove that argument incorrect and support my thesis. My story of individuals started with Pastor Jim, Nadine, and Jeremiah Bailey. The actions of three separate individuals changed my life, pulled me off the street, and then I made others' lives better through Christopher House. And yes, Christopher House is an organization, but it did not run without the individuals who directly worked with the people on the streets.

It was a struggle facing my life a year later. I felt like an entirely different person now, in a different life, separate from who I was before, almost as if the previous year I had played a character in a movie, two separate selves, one based in a present reality and one based in a past that no longer seemed real. I was moving forward and didn't feel like dredging up the memories. It was painful. But, as I struggled to form words on the screen, images came into focus and words began to flow.

My fingers slowly started pecking away at the keys. And after I began stringing a few words, then sentences, then paragraphs together, my fingers gained speed and my story began to take shape. The library lights began to shut down when it neared closing time on the third day. I peered at the bottom of the screen. I had written twenty pages. The remaining lights flickered overhead, a sign the library was closing in five minutes.

As I brought the memories of my past to the pages on the screen, my life felt like it was finally coming back into focus. I stood up, stretched my arms in the air, and let out a long, slow, cathartic breath. I reached over and shut down the computer. I gathered my stuff and headed out the front of the library. The brisk night air filled my lungs and fueled my walk home that night, a walk that suddenly felt more purposeful. I could now embrace the dark year of my life as just another experience, a tough one, but just another experience, nonetheless. While it did shape who I had become once I came out the other side, I was proud of my resolve and what it took for me to climb out of the hole and make it back to ground zero.

I was what I was because of what came before, but I was still in the process of working on who I would become in the days ahead, and I was ready for this new chapter of my life.

Chapter Four

The end of spring term came and went and summer term was bustling with possibilities. I struggled for the first month or so to integrate back into normal life. But, as I walked through campus—by the library where I spent many a day and night studying and working on the computers, while waiting for my new laptop to arrive, bought with money from my grants and student loans—through corridors that led to the many classrooms and meeting halls, I had a new sense of self. I was now fully part of the college scene. I was a student. I was an academic.

With my backpack full—my new laptop secure within—I walked with a feeling of excitement. The sun shone through the large intermittent windows in the corridors and created a pattern of speckled light on the gray tiled floors. Doors opened and closed along my journey as students came and went.

I found my first class of the semester in the third of three lecture halls situated on the south side of a large hallway in the main building at the center of campus. It was a fifteen-minute walk from my dorm. I pulled the large wooden door and heard the slow squeak of the hinges echo inside. I walked into the dimly lit room. It had two tiers of seats separated by a walkway in between. A few students sat spread apart from one another.

The sound of my footsteps bounced off the walls as I made my way in and looked for a seat. Heads turned my way, curious to see who was interrupting the silence.

I walked up the stairs that divided the balcony in half and found a seat in the fourth row. I pulled out my notepad and pen and set my laptop on the small table connected to a hinge on the right side of the seat. Over the next ten minutes, students began to file in and fill seats around the auditorium. A low murmur overtook the silence and life began to form in the room.

A few minutes later, a woman entered from the door to the right of the large whiteboard that filled half of the wall in the front. She turned and flicked a switch beside the door. Lights came on overhead. She turned to the board and scrawled her name and the name of the class in elegant hand—Margaret Jeffries, Psychology 102.

When I entered college the first time, I was set on a life of numbers. I was drawn to economics, to math-related endeavors, and to computers. But, ever since I made it back from my life that was disconnected from life, ever since I returned from the invisible life in which the world hovered around me unaware of my existence, I was pulled toward the social sciences. I was not quite sure what I wanted to focus on, but I did know that I was interested in learning more about the nature of human existence. This is where I separated my life as a child—the life where religion was forced upon us at home—from who I'd become. It didn't make sense to me that God would abandon me the way my parents did, but it sure felt that way. So, in order to make sense of it all, I put that part of my life out of my mind and focused on the more secular study of human development.

Soon, the auditorium was packed. I looked around and did a

quick calculation in my head—probably two hundred seats. A few students strained to find the last remaining spots.

I looked down by my feet and reached for a bottled water on the side of my backpack. When I lifted my head, I noticed one last student frantically turning his head from side to side, looking for a place to sit. I suddenly wished there was a seat beside me. His shoulder-length curls covered half his face, but when he flicked his head toward the balcony where I was sitting, I caught a glimpse—just enough. My heart rate quickened. My breathing shallowed. I felt the temperature in the room rise ten degrees.

"Good morning," a soft, yet firm voice filled the room. "Welcome to Human Development, Psychology 102. If you are here for Psych 403, they printed the wrong room number on some of the schedules. It's located directly across the hall in A204." A few students got up and hurried out and I wondered how they missed the large "Psychology 102" scrolled on the whiteboard.

"I'm Professor Jefferies. You can find my information on the University website listing my office hours and contact information." She continued to talk, but her voice trailed off as my attention was drawn to the brown, shoulder-length curls sitting in front of me. The late arriving student had found a seat two rows below where I was sitting. It was all I could do to pull my attention back to the professor at the front of the room and the forty-five-minute lecture became a daydream as my mind wandered in and out of a fantasy. I pictured myself walking up to him after class, introducing myself, and asking him to coffee. He accepted, and the dream continued from there. When class ended I sat motionless, watching him rise, walk down the stairs, turn left, and vanish from sight.

Class continued like that for two weeks, although I did manage to focus my attention on Professor Jefferies, at least enough to jot down pertinent information. I made sure I always showed up early enough to sit in the same seat, with a perfect view of the entrance. I kept my eyes peeled so I didn't miss him. He was always one of the last to show up, fortunately, there was always a seat two rows below mine. I spent a good part of the twice-a-week lecture watching him from afar and imagining how I would approach him after each class. But, I was also a little worried about talking to him and finding out he had a girlfriend. Ultimately, the lecture would end and I would sit and watch him leave. One day, though, as he entered class, he wore a tight pink shirt, cut just above his belly button, under a black leather jacket that sat above his hips. A large silver zipper ran down the center of his jacket and a thick belt with a large silver buckle dangled along the bottom. I closed my eyes and smiled. My confidence rose.

Chapter Five

Two weeks later, Joey, a friend I met earlier in the year, invited me and a couple other guys to a local bar off campus. The parking lot was full, so we parked a block away. The place was buzzing. Students were lined up outside waiting to open their wallets, show their IDs, and disappear into the strobing lights and booming music. Each time the door opened, the sights and sounds wafted out and met the quiet night. It was as if those of us outside were just waiting to glimpse a different world, even if just for a brief moment.

Thirty minutes passed. We were finally inside, overtaken by heart-pounding thuds, strobing lights, and the smell of beer and overactive hormones. We looked around to get our bearings and finally found a small slice of table crowded by a few students from the university. We stood in our own silence, forced upon us by the ravenous sounds of the garage band jamming on the small stage opposite the bar.

Joey turned to us, held up his hand, and took a swig of an imaginary drink. I read his lips as best I could, "I'll grab us some beers," was my interpretation. We watched as he dodged through the crowd, and, with not a little effort, finally found his way to the bar. I assumed it would be a decent wait before he'd be back, so I scanned the room to pass the time.

I recognized a few people scattered around the bar, a couple from one of my classes, and another I passed in the halls on the way to class every day. I peered onto the dance floor off to the left and saw a guy who lived in the dorm down the hall from me dancing with his hands over his head. I peered over to the corner of the bar next to a big speaker, probably four feet tall. From my vantage point, it looked to be vibrating as the music sprang from its innards. However, I couldn't be sure if it was the speaker or my eyeballs pinballing in their sockets as the vibrations of the music transferred from the floor into my legs and body and up to my head. And then, my eyes caught sight of a familiar figure leaning against the wall a few feet from the speaker. His brown curls covered his face. My heart skipped a beat, and again, just like the first time, I could feel the temperature in the room rise ten degrees as I recognized him as the guy sitting two rows below me in class.

Joey finally made it back, four beers in hand. He set them on the table. "Drink up," a muffled yell barely made it to our ears. We each picked up our drink. I took a swig and then looked back at the figure by the speaker. He was still there, leaning against the wall.

"I'll get the next round," I said. They looked back at me with confusion. "I'll get the next round," I yelled.

They nodded. Jeff leaned over and touched my hand. "Don't get me too drunk tonight," he winked.

"I'll try not to," I laughed. We relaxed for a few minutes listening to the music, watching the action on the dance floor. "Hey, guys—I'll be right back." I held up my index finger. Joey smiled. Tim nodded. Jeff sent me a concerned scowl, his hand still gently touching mine.

I walked over there, to where he was—the figure with the

curls I recognized from class. The room was crowded, people were moving haphazardly around trying to make their way from the entrance, along the dance floor, and to the bar on the other side of the room, so I had to sidle this way and that, holding my drink in my right hand, high above my head.

I kept my nerves steady while the boom-thud-boom-thud of the bass rattled through my body, shaking my organs, filling my head. I took a deep breath and tried to figure out what I was going to say, or more aptly, how I was going to say anything audible above the sound reverberating out of the monstrous speaker that was just a few feet away.

His brown, loose curls bounced softly on his shoulders as he leaned back against the wall and nodded to the rhythm of the music. I watched his hips sway softly to and fro, just slightly, as the thump of the bass vibrated through the floor, up my legs, and into my body, intensifying the feeling of nervous excitement welling inside me.

I stood next to him. His eyes were shut. He seemed to be enveloped by the music, letting it guide the movement of his body. I waited.

The music stopped. The pressure was released from the room. It took a few seconds to regain my senses enough to open my mouth and let words of greeting softly tiptoe upon the air. "Hello." I directed my comment to the dancing figure who was still leaning, eyes shut, against the wall. "Hello," I said again, a bit louder. He slowly opened his eyes and turned his head. A slight smile took shape at the corners of his mouth as his eyes fell upon me. "I recognize you from psych class," I said, my ear still recovering from the now-silent music. "I usually sit a couple rows above you." He nodded in recognition. "I was wondering if I could buy you a drink?" Suddenly we were rendered mute again by the squeal of an electric guitar and the boom-tick-boom-boom-tick of the drums.

He leaned over to my ear. "What's your name?" His breath warmed the side of my face and sent my heart racing. I turned my head and introduced myself in his ear. The quick exchange of intimacy was exhilarating. He returned the favor, "I'm Kelly." He smiled at me through the music. "I've seen you in class, too." We paused briefly as the music continued to fill the air.

"How 'bout that drink?" I asked again, continuing our intimate, abbreviated conversation. He nodded. I lifted my beer to my mouth, downed what was left, and tossed the bottle in a garbage can near the wall. I could have left him by the speaker while I ventured for our drinks, but I didn't want to miss my chance. I took his hand nervously. We traversed the sea of bodies and then wriggled our way in at the end of the bar. I put my hands on his shoulders and moved him in front of me to make room for both of us, then leaned over his shoulder. "What'll you have?"

He turned his head. His hair brushed against my face, "I'll take a Vodka on the rocks."

I took a deep breath to control my nerves and then reached into my pocket, pulled out a twenty-dollar bill, and waived it over my head. The bartender looked my way and nodded. "Two Vodka on the rocks and three beers," I yelled over the avalanche of notes bouncing off the walls.

We waited, music recoiling around us, my heart pounding, hands on his shoulders, my chest leaning against his back. The music stopped again. A communal sigh was felt throughout the room. "Wow. I can finally hear myself think," I said a bit too loudly. We both laughed. I pointed to the other side of the room, "Let's go over there. My friends and I have a table." He nodded, just as a softer music retook the room. Couples began moving slowly, seductively, to a low bass and a double stroke keeping beat softly on the high hat. I rifled through my pocket for another bill and set it alongside the twenty on the bar as our drinks were handed to us. We picked them up and worked our way to the table.

"Hey, guys... round two," I yelled as I set the drinks in front of them.

Jeff picked up his beer, a look of concern on his face. He turned toward me, "I see you brought someone with you," he added as he took a swig of his drink, lifted the back of his hand to his face, and wiped his mouth.

"Yeah... Guys, this is Kelly. We have the same psych class." They nodded. "Kelly, this is Joey, Jeff, and Tim."

"Nice to meet yuh," Kelly said, nodding his head in return.

The music blared on as it shifted back to a thumping fast-paced rhythm. I looked at Kelly and smiled. He reached over, softly took my hand, and leaned toward me, "I'm supposed to meet my friends soon."

"Oh—okay." We each took a sip of our drink and stood, the music filling the space between us. "It's not the best place to get to know each other," I said with an awkward giggle. "I just didn't want to pass on the opportunity to introduce myself."

"I'm glad you did." He took another sip of his drink, seductively looking at me over the rim of his glass.

I looked at him, trying to figure out how to extend this chance meeting beyond the night. "Maybe we can have lunch after class sometime."

"Sure. I'm usually hungry after Jeffries' lectures." He let out a sigh that failed to overtake the music, but penetrated my heart. We stood for a few minutes finishing our drinks, his hand softly holding mine.

"There they are." He gestured toward two guys and a girl near the front door.

"Can I walk you out?"

"Of course." He took one last sip, set his glass on the table, and waved at the guys. They nodded. He pulled at my hand and led me toward the door and then turned. "It was nice to meet you," once again whispering his hot breath into my ear.

"Yeah, I'll see you in class." I squeezed his hand, not wanting to let go, and then watched as he walked over to his friends. They stood for a bit, talking, and then disappeared out the door. I made my way back to the table. Joey and Tim were missing.

Jeff turned toward me and leaned over the table. "How long you known him?" he said, distorting his lips into an awkward frown.

"Just met him officially, but I've had my eye on him in class for a while," I remarked without reverence. He pursed his lips, a quizzical look on his face. I didn't think more of it—then turned my attention to the middle of the room. Joey and Tim were dancing with a couple girls I hadn't seen before. I looked back at the table and noticed an empty bottle in Jeff's hand. "I'm almost done with my drink," I said over the din of the music. "You want another one?"

"Not sure," he replied sharply, staring off into the flashing lights above the dance floor. "One of us has to drive home."

"I'll grab a couple more beers. You can make your decision when I get back."

I waded through the crowd once more and ordered my drinks at the bar. I turned toward our table as I waited. Jeff was no longer there. I looked at the mass of bodies on the dance floor.

Joey and Tim were in the middle keeping rhythm with the music. Jeff was nowhere. I looked around the room and didn't see him. I took a deep breath and let it out slowly. I put two elbows on the bar and put my head in my hands. The music blared around me and suddenly felt uncomfortably loud.

My drinks arrived. I looked up and smiled at the bartender and then turned around and leaned my back on the bar. Jeff was still gone. I took a slow drink of my beer and looked around the room. I didn't see him anywhere.

I walked back to the table and waited. The music stopped momentarily. Joey and Tim walked off the dance floor, big smiles on their faces, laughing.

"Where's Jeff," Joey asked between bouts of laughter.

"Don't know. Went to get us some beers and he was gone."

"Huh... hope he returns. He's our ride home," Tim quipped.

"Well, I've got a beer up for grabs if you want to fight over it." I set it on the table. They both eyed it. Joey smiled and shrugged.

Tim reached over, "Don't mind if I do," and took a swig.

We stood there as the music rose and overtook our conversation. I looked at my watch. *Almost midnight,* I thought to myself. Joey and Tim leaned on the table and looked out at the dance floor, smiles of contentment on their faces. I, on the other hand, had a knot in my stomach.

I suddenly felt sick. The music was overwhelming and felt like it was closing in on me. My blood coursed through my body and pounded in rhythm with the bass that bounced inside my head. I placed my palms flat on the table, braced myself, closed my eyes, and took two slow breaths. The pounding in my head softened and my heart rate slowed down.

For some reason I felt like I did something wrong, that I had done something to offend Jeff, but what did it matter? I hardly knew him anyway. I really didn't even know why he suddenly went missing. Maybe he felt the call of nature and was stuck in the bathroom. And Joey and Tim didn't seem to care. So, what's the big deal?

I opened my eyes. Joey and Tim were standing quietly, looking out at the dance floor, the empty beer bottle sitting on the table. I leaned over, "You guys ready to head out?" I watched as my muffled voice barely made it to them. They looked at each other and shrugged. Joey smiled and gave me a thumbs-up. "Maybe Jeff's out front," I said as I motioned my head toward the door.

We made our way outside, weaving through a thinning crowd of beer-crazed college students, and looked around the parking lot. We were met by the soft hum of the neon sign above the entrance and a cooling breeze, yet it still felt like I had corks loosely tamped in my ears.

"Humm... Don't see him," Tim said.

"Well, we can always call a Lyft," Joey replied.

As we stood in the parking lot in the wee hours of what was once a promising night, heads turning this way and that, searching for a way home, a truncated beep-beep caught our attention. "Hey guys, let's go," Jeff's impatient come hither drew us to the car.

"Maybe we should have checked the car," Tim said, as he shook his head in disgust.

"Yeah, right," Joey huffed.

We trudged over to the car and found Jeff, seat reclined behind the wheel, window down, humming along with some soft rock.

Joey reached in the window and playfully slapped Jeff on the face, "Wake up, knucklehead?"

Tim rounded the front of the car and hopped in the passenger seat, "Whatcha doin'? We thought you took off."

"I probably should have. Thought you two were going home with those girls. Looked like you were getting along pretty good."

Joey peered at me from the other side of the car. "He gets like this sometimes. A bit self-absorbed." We jumped in the back seat. Joey pounded the headrest in front of him. "Put your fucken seat up so I have some room." Jeff released the knob under his seat and it raised with a sudden thud.

We drove off. An ominous silence filled the car. I sat there wondering what prompted the sudden mood swing. Less than an hour ago we were crammed in the local bar with half the student body having a great time. Now, a wet blanket had been thrown over the fire.

A few minutes later, we came to a screeching stop in front of a run-down fourplex. Joey and Tim hopped out. Joey slammed the back door and then leaned in the window toward me. "Don't be a stranger, man. See yuh around." He pulled his head out and pounded his hand twice on the top of the car." Jeff hit the gas and we took off with a jerk.

"Thanks for driving tonight," I said, trying to fill the void, yet my words lingered in the air unanswered. Jeff reached out and turned up the music. We continued in silence until we came to a hard stop in front of my dorm. "Thanks for the ride," I said as I unbuckled my seatbelt. "Let's do it again," I forced myself to say. I noticed a slight nod as I stared at the back of Jeff's head. "Okay—have a good night," I stepped out of the car and shut the door with a thud that acted as an exclamation point to a night that took an unexpected turn to awkwardness. I stood for a moment watching the car move off into the darkened night and then I took a deep breath and shrugged my shoulders with a feeling of confusion.

Lying in bed that night, I ran the events of the evening through my head. Did I imagine the shift in Jeff's attitude toward me? Maybe I was making more out of it than there really was. Joey did say Jeff gets self-absorbed after a couple drinks. I finally drifted off as I shifted my thoughts from the awkward ending to the chance encounter with the handsome brown-haired guy from my psych class. I quietly whispered his name to myself several times hoping to prompt my dreams to become fantasies.

Chapter Six

I was sitting on a bench outside the lecture hall watching students file in. Normally I would be one of the first few students settling into my seat, getting out my laptop, and logging into the school's Wi-Fi, but today I worked to act naturally as I waited for Kelly to scurry in just before the beginning of class. I kept my eyes peeled down the hall so I could watch him walking. It seemed like an eternity since we met at the bar just three days ago. I took a quick, shallow breath and blew it out, hoping to calm my nerves, yet my heart seemed to ignore my wishes. And then I caught a glimpse of him walking among the hustle and bustle of students rushing into lecture halls on either side of the corridor. He didn't see me as he walked confidently, eyes glued to his phone.

"Excuse me, sir," I said in jest as he got close enough to hear my voice. "Do you have the time?"

He looked up unknowingly, eyebrows raised, and then a smile of recognition appeared on his face. "Hello again," he said.

"Hey," I replied, "Mind if we sit together?"

"We might be hard-pressed finding two seats together at this point, but we can try."

We made our way in and scanned the room, luckily finding two seats at the very top. I held my hand out. He stepped in front of me and I watched him climb the stairs, and then, for most of the next forty-five minutes, we appeared to be focused on note-taking. However, neither of us could help stealing a few glances at each other now and then. Time seemed to last forever and the words coming from the front of the classroom could not seem more irrelevant at the moment. I labored to jot down as many notes as I could and, later that night, when I was studying in the library and reading them back, I could tell my focus was elsewhere.

When class ended and students began to file out, we sat, not saying a word. And then I broke the silence. "You wanna get some lunch?"

"I'd love to, but I can't today. I have to meet a friend in a little bit."

"How 'bout after next class?" I asked as I reached over and put my hand on his.

"Yeah, sure. I have a two-hour break before my afternoon class on Thursday."

"Can I walk you somewhere today?"

"I'm meeting my friend at the library if you wanna head that way."

We spent the next fifteen minutes meandering through campus discovering that we had probably crossed paths over the past few months walking to classes, to and from our dorms which sit kitty-corner from each other on the Westside of campus, and most likely eating lunch at the pub in the quad. And then we said our goodbyes as we reached the library. I headed to the pub for a bite to eat after I watched him turn and walk through the revolving glass doors and vanish out of sight. I sat with a coffee and bagel and pictured myself walking past him numerous times on my way around campus while looking forward to our upcoming lunch on Thursday.

For the next two months, we spent an hour together after each class either getting lunch in the pub or just sitting and sipping coffee at one of a few stands scattered around campus. We spent a couple Friday and Saturday nights together, as well, going to movies and dinner.

Our relationship had not progressed to anything serious. We just enjoyed our time getting to know each other. We walked freely together—not holding hands or displaying any physical affection. Our time together was relaxed and our conversation flowed easily and we found out we had a lot in common. We both played football in high school and attended the obligatory Senior Prom with our female dates, awkwardly kissing at the end of the night as we dropped our dates off at their front doors. It seemed as if he followed my exact path through high school just two years after I blazed that uncomfortable trail. We were both at the end of our college freshman year, but I was sidetracked by my time on the street and at Christopher House.

We did find one blaring difference between us, however. While neither of our parents took the news of our coming out in the best light, his parents eventually came around. He said his dad is still a bit uncomfortable with the idea, but he is working through it. I shared how my parents abandoned me and I was unable to pay for school and ended up on the streets. He was heartbroken, and for the first time we touched, as he put his hand on my knee. We sat in the sun, sipping the lattes we had made a habit of purchasing together the last few weeks, and shared a quiet moment.

Chapter Seven

A soft intermittent buzz pulled my concentration from the textbook I was trying to work my way through to my phone sitting atop my mini-fridge. I reached over, hoping it was Kelly, but to my surprise, my parents' number showed on the screen. I wasn't sure how they found my number. I had just gotten my cell phone a couple weeks ago and only gave it to a few people. I stared at the phone and watched as it tickled my hand, not sure if I was going to answer. But, with an uncomfortable breath, I tapped the green button and put it to my ear. "Hello?" I said tentatively.

"Hi," a quiet voice replied on the other end.

"Mom?"

"How are you?" she asked, a slight quiver in her voice.

I paused—not knowing how to respond—and cleared my throat. "How'd you get my number?" I asked abruptly.

"Your sister gave it to me."

"Ah—okay—I'm doing fine. How's she doing?"

"She had Senior Prom last weekend."

"That's cool."

"Yeah—yeah—she had a good time," she stammered.

I could tell she was working up to something. I could tell there was more to this first call in over nine months than telling me my sister went to prom. "So, what's up?"

"I'm just calling to see how you're doing?"

"Right—okay—well—like I said, I'm fine."

"That's good." The phone went silent for a long moment. "Your dad asked about you the other day."

"O—kay?" I replied with hesitation.

"He wanted to know if you were going to pick up those last couple boxes of your stuff from the garage."

"You mean he wants to get rid of anything that reminds him of me."

"No—he was just wondering."

"Sure—I'll come by in the next few days. Just leave them on the porch so I don't disturb you."

"No—really—it's okay. We'd love to see you."

My patience started wearing thin. "So, was that it? You just want me to clear your life of all my stuff?"

"Well, actually..."

It was all I could do to keep my cool. "Actually, what?"

"Your dad's in the hospital."

"What do you mean, he's in the hospital?" I shook my head. I knew there was something more

"He had a stroke two days ago and is recovering."

"Hmmm." I paused. "What do you want me to say?"

"Nothing really. I just wanted you to know."

"Is he going to live?"

"Yes." She cleared her throat. "But it will take a while for him to recover—and he won't be the same."

"So, it must have been a big one."

"Yeah," her voice trailed off. "Pretty severe."

"That's too bad." I fought myself from showing any emotion, but could feel my voice shaking.

"I was hoping you would come visit him."

"I'm pretty busy with classes right now."

"It would mean a lot to him."

"Are you sure? Won't me being there make it more difficult on him?"

"No—no—he would love to see you."

"What time are visiting hours?"

"Nine to eleven in the morning and two to four in the afternoon."

"I'm not sure, but I'll see if I can fit it in."

"It would mean a lot."

"To who?" I heard my raised voice crack.

"Come on son. Don't you want to see your father?"

"It's not my top priority, but I'll look at my schedule."

"Okay, well, I hope to see you soon."

"Yeah, maybe." I shook my head as I hung up the phone and sat on my bed, silently, trying to calm my nerves. "What the fuck is she thinking?" I asked the empty room. I laid my head back on my pillow and stared blankly at the ceiling. I closed my eyes and then turned over on my side and picked up the phone again.

"Hello?"

"Hey, Kelly."

"You miss me already?" his voice sparkled.

"Well, yeah, but I'm actually calling because I have a favor to ask."

"Sure. What's up?"

"My dad's in the hospital."

"Oh…" he replied, a sweetness enveloping his voice. "What happened?"

"He had a stroke and it sounds pretty bad."

"Sorry to hear that," he said softly.

"I was wondering if you'd go to the hospital with me."

"Oh, yeah—sure—when?"

"Maybe tomorrow after psych class. You'd have to miss your afternoon class, though."

"I can swing that. I'll get the lecture notes online."

"Thanks. I appreciate it. I haven't talked to my dad since before I was living on the streets. I'm not even sure he wants to see me."

"I'm sure he does, but I'll be there with you either way."

That night I went to bed confused, emotion grappling with reason. If I followed my first instinct I would avoid seeing my dad at all costs, but the logical side of my brain knew I needed to go, just in case it was the last time I saw him. The only real consolation was that Kelly would be with me because I wasn't sure I could face my dad alone. I finally fell asleep, a tight knot wreaking havoc in the pit of my stomach, much like the one I had almost every night I fell asleep on the cold cement in the middle of the bustling city.

Chapter Eight

When the morning came, I thought I might be sick, but after I sat up and allowed myself to wake, I knew last night's knot was still taking up space in my stomach. My first instinct was to lay back down and sleep through the day, but I forced myself to get up. I sat on the edge of my bed for a few minutes thinking about what I would say to my dad as I entered his hospital room. I wondered what he would look like. Not only had I not seen him in over two years, the stroke had probably affected his face.

I finally stood up and got ready for the impending day, showering, eating a small yogurt, downing the last half of an OJ that was on the door of my mini fridge, and brushing my teeth. Thirty minutes later I was sitting in the middle of psych class, saving a seat for Kelly, a ritual we had started after the first day sitting together. Yet, as class started and the professor began her introductory remarks, he hadn't arrived. I wondered if he had gotten cold feet and really didn't want to go with me to see my dad. But five minutes later, he scurried in and found his seat next to me.

"What'd I miss?" he whispered, out of breath.

"Not much," I whispered back, my heart pounding in relief. "She said today's lecture would go over the main points on the midterm."

"Sounds fun," he said with a breathless laugh.

I worked hard focusing on the professor's voice and keeping the nauseating thought of visiting my father out of mind. By the end of class, I felt pretty good about my note-taking, but at the same time, the knot started to form in the pit of my stomach again. Students filtered out while I sat there trying to gain the nerve to begin my trek toward the man who allowed me to be kicked out of school and set adrift on the streets—the man who once claimed to be my father, my provider, my protector.

"You okay?" a calming voice fluttered my way. I turned. Kelly was smiling softly. "I'm sure you're nervous, but I'll be there with you."

I smiled back and took an audible breath. "If we're going to do this, we might as well get going."

We walked across campus, dropped our backpacks off at our dorms, and then made our way to the parking lot where Kelly's blue Toyota Corolla was waiting. "You want some music?" Kelly asked as he turned over his right shoulder and backed the car out of its spot. "Relax a bit. Find a good station." He turned back around, righted the car, and started us on our way.

I tapped my right hand on my leg as a soft rhythm filled the car—it wouldn't have mattered the song, my hand moved instinctively as my mind was in another world and I looked out the window in a daze, anonymous buildings and cars flying by on either side. The knot in my stomach was dissipating, yet I could still feel a faint murmur of pent-up energy fluttering about, a reminder of the upcoming confrontation. While I wasn't sure what the confrontation would entail, I knew it would be some sort of confrontation with the man who is known as my father, who lay in a hospital bed recovering from a life-altering trauma. If nothing else, it would be a confrontation with emotion—emotion that I thought I had put behind me a few months ago, that had now resurfaced.

"You're awfully quiet," Kelly said as the current song came to an end. He reached over and turned down the volume. "Do you want to talk?"

"Probably should." A nervous chuckle escaped my lips. "I'm not sure what to expect. I don't even know if he is awake or if he can recognize anything."

"Well, do you have anything you want to say to him?"

"Not really. I put everything behind me so I could survive. I didn't have the time or the strength to think about anything else."

"And now?" He gave me a second to respond. "Does this change any of that?"

"You mean is everything still behind me?" I waited before I answered. "I wish it was." I shook my head. "When I woke up I thought I was sick. I hadn't felt that way for a while."

"Just take it slow and see how it goes. If you don't want to stay very long, we can take off whenever you want. You don't owe him anything."

By the time we reached the hospital, my nerves had mostly subsided. I can't say I was looking forward to seeing my dad, but I can say I knew I would at least survive the visit. I knew I had been through much tougher circumstances over the past couple years—a small consolation of my time on the streets.

We arrived a few minutes before visiting hours and took a seat in the waiting room by the third-floor intensive care unit. It was eerily quiet. Three large, floor-to-ceiling windows flooded the room with light and the hustle and bustle of the city was visible below, an added juxtaposition to the lifelessness that filled the room. I walked over to the window and leaned forward, resting my forehead against the clear pain of glass that separated me from life below. I could see people walking on the sidewalks and cars going up and down the road. I looked up and watched the white clouds float through blue skies. The sun was at its peak and reflected off the silver window of the building directly across. A small plane disappeared and then reappeared as if flew behind the steeple of a church off in the distance.

I looked down at my watch. It was two o'clock. The time of reckoning was here—time to face what I thought I had separated from—what I thought I had put behind me. I walked over to Kelly who was reading an old magazine he found on a side table in the waiting room. "You ready?"

He looked up. "Sure. How 'bout you?"

I smiled, took his hand, and we walked through a set of swinging doors that read, *Intensive Care—Quiet—No Cell Phones*. We looked at the numbers on the first two rooms—IC 2001, IC 2002. I took a piece of paper out of my pocket and read IC 2006. Further down the hall, the door was half open and a dim light struggled to make its way out. I looked down at our joined hands, took a breath, and shook my head slowly. Kelly squeezed my hand once and shot me a smile. I nodded, pushed the door open gently, and peered in. There were two beds. The bed closest to the door was vacant. A line of light made its way through drawn curtains and fell near my dad's feet at the end of the second bed near the far wall. My mom was sitting in a chair in the corner, head leaning back, eyes closed. I cleared my throat. She opened her eyes, a look of surprise—and then a smile emerged on her face. She stood up and walked toward me. She looked at me and then at Kelly and then down at our clasped hands. With tears in her eyes and without words, she reached out and embraced me.

"Thanks for coming." She held me for a moment longer and then stepped back. "Who's your friend?"

"This is Kelly." They exchanged smiles. "How's dad?"

"He sleeps a lot, but wakes up periodically and can talk a bit."

"I don't want to disturb him," I said nervously.

"It's okay. He'll be glad you're here." She turned to look at him. "Let me see if I can get him to open his eyes." She walked over to the far side of the bed and whispered in his ear. "Honey, your son is here." She paused, looked at him, and then held his hand. "Your son is here," she whispered again.

A muffled groan, barely audible. He moved his lips and his eyes fluttered slightly. He took a deep, labored breath and let it out. He turned his head slightly and opened his eyes.

I walked toward him, Kelly in tow. I squeezed Kelly's hand as I reached out and put my free hand on my dad's shoulder. "Can you see me?" My first words to my dad since my coming out party was crashed by his silence two years ago.

"Yeah. I—" He stopped and took a shallow breath and then whispered, "I can see you."

Words struggled on my lips. "Are you comfortable?"

"Sure." He turned his head a bit more. "Who's this?" he asked, with his usual gruffness, frowning toward the stranger holding my hand.

"This is Kelly, Dad"

"Hmmmm..." a note of—I'm not sure—emoted from deep within his bowels. Was it concern? Was it disgust? I didn't know if he could be discerning enough to have an opinion. Maybe it was just a note of recognition.

"Kelly's in my psych class. We've known each other for a couple months. He gave me a ride here."

"Ahh—Okay," He said through labored breaths.

"We've been spending a lot of time together."

An animated sigh rose from his otherwise emotionless face.

"What's that dad?" I was suddenly agitated. I wanted to question him. I wanted to raise my voice and release the pent-up emotions that were lying under the surface of my skin. *Do you have a problem with that—Do you have a problem with me?* I wasn't sure if I was reading too much into the situation, but I couldn't help feeling irritated.

I felt a gentle tug on my hand. I turned toward Kelly. "It's okay," he mouthed.

I took a breath and stood silently for a moment. "Well." I looked down at my feet and then back at the figure in the bed. "Well, I'll call tomorrow and check in on you."

Silence.

"Okay then." I looked over at my mom, eyebrows raised, silently asking what to do next. She looked back, but offered nothing. I pulled Kelly toward the door.

"Hey," my dad's raspy voice met me before I could leave. I turned. "Don't call," he said with what little strength he had left, his vacant stare glued to the ceiling.

I shook my head and walked out, pulling Kelly quickly into the hall. I looked at him and breathed out what felt like toxic fumes that had been locked deep in my lungs for years. He looked, tilted his head, and gave me a knowing smile. We rode the elevator in silence and found our way to his car, the brief visit now in the past. On our way home, Kelly helped me process my feelings. By the time we were parked in front of our dorms, I had made a decision. All ties had been severed and I could move on. My dad's final words and my mom's inability to speak up allowed me to fully and completely step away from that relationship and move on with my life. I didn't want to give

49

myself a chance to feel bad. I didn't want to allow the experience to dampen my spirits or pull me from my current path. I was determined to continue moving forward, just as determined as I was to get off the street less than a year ago. I had righted my ship, and at this point, that is all that mattered.

Chapter Nine

The next morning, I was oddly relaxed. It was Friday. I had one morning class at nine-thirty and then the weekend. I sat on the end of my bed, gnawing on the second half of yesterday's protein bar, and then got up and readied myself for the day.

Before class, I stopped at a coffee stand and sat in the early morning sun drinking my usual latte, watching students scurry past. Off in the distance, I saw Joey, Jeff, and Tim sitting on a bench. I had only seen Joey and Tim briefly a couple of times since that fateful night at the bar, but hadn't talked to Jeff at all. I cocked my head and watched as they joked and laughed, and then stood and walked toward them, my curiosity getting the best of me.

"Hey, guys," I said as I approached, hand raised in greeting.

"How's it going?" Joey shot back.

"Good. What you guys up to?"

"Just killing time before class," Joey replied.

"Mind if I join yuh?"

"Sure," Joey stood up and moved his bag from the bench. "Take a seat."

I took off my backpack, sat down, and placed it at my feet. I leaned forward and looked to my left. "How you guys doin'?" I asked, addressing Jeff and Tim.

Tim nodded and mumbled through a mouth full of food, "Good."

Jeff sat, eyes looking the opposite way, and then stood up. "I'll see you guys in class," he said matter-of-factly, and walked off.

"Don't mind him. He doesn't know what he's doing," Tim said apologetically.

I smiled and took a drink of my latte. *Yup*, I thought to myself. *I knew there was some friction there.*

"How're your classes going?" Joey asked me.

"I really like my psych class. I could do without philosophy, though."

"I could never get the hang of philosophy," Tim laughed. "Doing much better with logic. Seems to make more sense."

"I haven't taken logic. Maybe I should give that a try."

"Not saying it's my favorite, but at least I understand it," Tim laughed.

Joey put his hand on my shoulder and looked at me a bit suspiciously, "Isn't your psych class where you met Kelly?"

"Yeah," I smiled.

"More than one reason to like that class then," Joey joked, giving me a playful shove on the shoulder. "How's that going, anyway? You guys still seeing each other?"

"We're still spending time together," I clarified. "We haven't made anything official."

"That's cool," he nodded and then looked at his watch. "Ah, we should get to class. We'll have to hang out again."

"Sounds good," I replied. "Maybe Jeff can hang around a bit longer next time," I winked.

They both shrugged. "Who knows with him," Joey added.

* * *

That evening I met Kelly at his dorm at six. With just two weeks left in the term, we had decided to let loose before we buckled down and spent the next ten days up in the library, writing term papers, and studying for our final exams. So, we went out to dinner and then to an alternative club a couple miles from campus. It wasn't strictly for LGBTQIA+, but if you were living some sort of life outside what people considered mainstream, you probably found your way to this club.

We found a nice side street bistro just after the dinner rush that wasn't too crowded, a couple blocks away from our destination. We ordered appetizers and picked at them for the next hour and a half as we sat at a sidewalk table and watched people and cars pass by. The sun was visible when we sat down and was now tucked nicely behind the buildings on the far side of the street, yet the sky was still illuminated, a darkening blue with pink-clouded highlights.

Nightlife in the city was always interesting, especially on Fridays and Saturdays. The tone slowly morphed from the hustle and bustle of roadwork, well-dressed business people scurrying about, coffee in hand, and the blaring horns of drivers darting in and out of traffic to what I would call a chill, laid-back ambiance of the nightcrawlers. A little ominous, a bit edgy, yet very compelling.

Clubs didn't open until nine, so we paid our bill and decided to take a walk and partake in the nightlife. We went a block west, hand in hand, past one of the more established homeless encampments, something that had become more and more a part of the developing street culture over the past decade. I winced as we turned the corner and almost ran into a man urinating on the wall of a mini-mart. I was not surprised or taken aback. I winced as reality washed over me and a pang of sorrow flowed through my veins. Ever since I wrote my first midterm paper back in college, "The Invisible Masses: Walking Passed Humanity," I had done everything I could to stay away from that blip in my life's trajectory—pushing memories deep down and out of mind. I had been treating that time of my life as an anomaly, something that would never happen again. When anything jarred my memory it would feel like an out-of-body experience—that wasn't real, maybe it wasn't really me—a scene from a movie perhaps. And while in reality, it was less than a year ago that I was working my way out of a homeless shelter, it had seemed like a lifetime ago, until now.

A lump formed in my throat as we walked past an established frontier of tents that lined both sides of the alleyway right off the main sidewalk. I didn't want to look in, but also couldn't help myself. The darkening night brought with it an almost apocalyptic overtone as shadowy figures lingered near garbage cans of rising embers and makeshift homes for two blocks.

We continued walking, although I couldn't help but feel drawn back to the encampment. "Hold on," I said, stopping under a streetlamp and letting go of his hand.

"What's up?"

"I can't do it."

"What do you mean?"

"Do you remember the term paper I told you about—the one about my time on the streets?"

"Yes," he replied, an odd look of intrigue on his face.

"I can't do it. I can't just walk past. I can't treat them like they are invisible."

"So, what do you want to do?"

"I'm not sure, but I know I have to do something." I reached out and grabbed Kelly's hand. "I can't continue to pretend it never happened, that it was not me waking up on the cold cement, scrounging through dumpsters for meals."

"I'm sorry." He pulled me close and gave me a long hug. He let go and put both hands on my shoulders and looked me in the eyes. "I'm sorry you had to experience that."

"It's time I stopped hiding. The only way I can truly move on is by going back—by giving back." I took a deep breath and looked up at the forming stars in the sky and then back at Kelly. "These are people. They are human beings. I was one of them. I am still one of them. I'll always be one of them. I can't forget that. I can't forget them." I started to feel angry. I started to feel frightened. I started to feel relief. Emotions welled up inside me and I began to shake ever so softly.

I took Kelly's hand and led him to the alleyway. We stopped and looked. I led him in and through without a word—listening and experiencing—taking in the pungent odor—the crackling fires—muffled words being spoken. We exited at the other end, after two blocks. We turn and look back. "That was me. That was what my home was like." Kelly stood there silently—next to me. He held tightly to my hand. Darkness enveloped the night, yet I saw clearly—we saw clearly. We stood for a long time—neither of us willing to let go of this moment—neither of us really knowing what we should do next. But one thing I did know—it felt like a turning point.

Silently, we began walking toward the club, sounds of the night accompanied us along the way—a screeching car in the distance, a group of unfamiliar voices passing on our left, a distorted bass pounding through the closed doors of a parked car, the pungent smell of marijuana floating through the air.

For some reason, it all felt right. For some reason it was comforting. I had not only been here before, I had lived here and then made my way out, and now it was a part of who I am. It was in my DNA and I felt like I could—and probably should—embrace it. I didn't quite know what that meant, but I felt more in tune with myself than I had ever been up until that point.

A block from the club we saw the bright lights of the illuminated sign and the thump of the music beckoned us forward. A gaggle of people hovered in front of the door. We joined the procession and slowly filed in. The bouncer checked our IDs and passed us through the door toward a dimly lit blue light that guided us through a hallway lined with shadowy images of dancers painted on the wall. At the end of the short corridor, a series of colorful strobes met the blue light, reminding me of a portal to another world.

We stepped through the portal and that is exactly what it was, a world I had never encountered before. At first, I was tempted to look at my watch to see if time had stopped, but I didn't want to spoil the wonderment. If time had stopped, I didn't want it to start again.

A bit thunderstruck, and without knowing what else to do, we walked slowly toward the bar. The club was packed, yet there was plenty of room to move around. We ordered our first round of drinks and savored them as we allowed ourselves to experience the sights and sounds. We stood. We watched. We turned to each other and smiled. It was unlike any place either of us had ever been. Unlike when I went out with Joey, Jeff, and Tim, the music was loud, but not overwhelming. While we weren't conversing on a normal level, we were able to hear each other and talk comfortably.

I recognized a few faces from campus or at least I thought I did. Some people were dressed in costume. Others dressed as they normally did. So, who really knew? One thing was clear, though. Here, people were who they were. This was a place people felt safe to express themselves.

We finished our drinks and found ourselves a seat at a booth opposite the bar, on the far side of the dance floor. At the moment we were content taking it all in—watching—listening—being together. We sat, occasionally sharing words, making comments, laughing. We kept rhythm with the music, heads nodding. We held hands.

I looked at my watch. It was already ten-thirty. "Maybe we should check out the dance floor before it gets much later," I said, sidling out of the booth and offering him my hand. He popped to his feet and followed me to the legion of bodies bouncing around in the middle of the room. We squeezed ourselves into the churning mass and were immediately inducted into their swarm. A seductive club mix mounted the air and sent electronic vibrations through our bodies. I had never really been one to dance freely in front of anyone, but at this moment I moved and gyrated, lost in the moment—lost in the freedom to be myself—lost in the freedom of a night in which I took control over myself, past and present.

We began moving in close proximity, moving on our own, giving ourselves time to find our rhythm, but soon, we were holding hands. I stroked his fingers with mine, as our hips moved with the music. I reached out with my other hand and softly touched the back of his arm and pulled him toward me. We moved in sync, pelvis to pelvis, back and forth, grinding softly against each other. The music played continuously as our bodies moved as one. Sweat was forming on the nap of my neck and my lower back, drops of perspiration slowly slithered down my spine.

I let go of his arm, put my hand on the back of his head, and caressed his neck. I slowly guided his face toward mine. Our lips touched. I felt his tongue explore my mouth and tasted the roasted malt of beer on his breath. I had never kissed another man before and at that moment I never wanted to kiss anyone else. The diluted smell of his cologne mixed with the heat of his body made the hairs on my arms stand on end. The music died down as the DJ announced the next song and the crowd erupted. The mass of bodies continued to convulse, moving rhythmically back and forth. We stayed embraced and then Kelly leaned a little closer and whispered in my ear, "What a night, huh?" He wrapped his arms around my neck.

"Yeah, wish we knew about this place a little sooner."

"It's intoxicating." He stepped back and twirled in a circle.

"You want another drink?" I asked as a slow rhythm enveloped the dance floor.

"Sure, why not."

I led him to the bar. We downed a couple shots and then we each grabbed a beer. We sat for a few minutes, catching our breath, watching the action.

"Who knew that life could be this fun," I said.

"Yup—It would be nice to have it like this every day."

"How 'bout we plan on coming back after finals?"

"I'm game." He closed his eyes and swayed to the music.

A little after midnight we decided to head out, making our way through the blue-lit corridor—passed an impassioned couple devouring each other against the darkened wall—and then made our way through the front door. We were expecting to be met by the quiet night, but instead were met by a group of college students dancing in their own little scrum, bouncing around and singing under the streetlight. I looked over to get a closer look, feeling compelled to join in, when I recognized one of them. I squinted—I looked—I tilted my head in disbelief. I stepped closer, pulling Kelly with me. I stood and listened. I heard his voice. Even dressed as he was, in a light blue tank top and black tights, I knew who he was.

"Jeff," I called over the cavalcade of noise. He didn't hear me. I let go of Kelly's hand and looked at him, "Just a minute. I want to say hi to someone."

I walked up to the group and made my way in—nobody noticing the one extra body. I put my hand on Jeff's shoulder and said his name again. He turned—his eyes widened. "Hey," I said energetically. He was silent.

He stuttered a less than enthusiastic retort. "Uh—hey—"

"How's it going?"

"Fine," he said, looking around nervously.

"Just wanted to say hi," I replied, offering him a warm smile. Seeing he was uncomfortable, I turned to go. I took a couple steps away, then turned back, "See you around campus." But my valediction floated on the air unanswered. He was gone.

I walked back to Kelly. "Who was that?" he asked.

I took his hand and gave him a disappointed smirk. "Just a guy I met a few months ago." I turned and stole a last look at the scrum bouncing around, singing to the night. But Jeff was still nowhere in sight.

We walked through the abandoned streets. I listened as the singing grew quiet, faint, and then disappeared. I couldn't help but wonder what was going on with Jeff, his swift change in attitude when he learned I was gay—and then, tonight, in his tight pants and tank top.

The next morning I woke up struggling to share the blanket

that wasn't meant for two. Kelly was still asleep beside me on my single bed, snug between me and the wall. It had been an interesting night. I revisited the events in my head—walking passed, and then through, the two blocks of makeshift homes and nameless people—dancing at the club—holding Kelly close as we moved to the music—and then the unexpected encounter with Jeff. Waking up with Kelly, I couldn't get Jeff out of my mind. I was confused, not sure what was up with Jeff, but also not sure why I cared.

I got up and turned on the coffee maker in the corner of the room and then walked back over and sat on the edge of the bed. I looked at Kelly as he slept. Last night was a whirlwind. We spent the last few months together hanging out, maybe just a little more than friends. But, on the dance floor, we were overtaken by the atmosphere. We were drawn together. It felt like a culmination of our relationship—of what we felt we had to do. We were together—we were gay—it was inevitable. But sitting there on the edge of the bed watching him cuddled under the blanket I knew the passion was left on the dance floor.

Kelly woke up and we sat together, quietly coming alive over two cups of coffee. We spent the morning talking about the moment on the dance floor. It was tantalizing and we both felt like we had found something we had been searching for forever, yet we both knew it wasn't really what we wanted. We both felt like we had experienced the night with a friend. And while we both enjoyed it, we felt the spark was not romantic, it was circumstantial—music, dancing, the flashing lights, and finally being with like-minded people.

As we sat at the small table next to the bed quietly sipping our coffee, knowing there wasn't a passionate connection, we looked at each other quietly. And then I pursed my lips—"Well, last night was an experience."

"It sure was." He looked at me sweetly.

The minutes passed. "So," I breathed in—and then out. "Whatcha thinking?"

"Hmm—well—the kiss was nice."

"Nice, huh?" I chuckled and looked into my cup.

"Well, nothing like I've ever experienced before." Our eyes met momentarily.

And suddenly we began to open up. We shared our feelings about each other. We shared how we both valued our friendship—and then, we shared how we became aware of our sexuality, years ago, as teenagers. I'm not quite sure how it happened, but it felt like the floodgates opened and it just came pouring out. He told me he was at a party in high school and saw two guys kissing and was aroused. He didn't know then, but over the next couple of years, it became apparent that he was attracted to guys. He never pursued relationships until after graduation because there was never really any opportunity and he never really told anyone, although he was sure others were suspicious.

I told him about my life as an athlete—about how I could have played college football if it weren't for a knee injury. "It was actually a relief. I didn't want to stay in the testosterone-driven life of a high-performing athlete. It wasn't who I was." I told him my hair-raising realization came in the seventh inning of our district championship game in high school, when, while sitting in the dugout next to our shortstop, a kid I had known for years, our arms touched and the hair on the back of my neck stood on end and a funny feeling gurgled up in my stomach. "I thought I was going to throw up. And for the next two years, all the way through graduation, I couldn't look at him without getting that tingling feeling in my stomach." I also told him about my many dates with girls and how "a long kiss with Sheila Williams on prom night didn't change my feelings at all."

We both expressed our relief with a shared sigh. It was a moment of clarity—a moment that seemed to release the pressure of years of repressed feelings.

"Okay," I said with an air of both relief and uncertainty. "What next?"

"Well, I—I'm not quite sure," Kelly chuckled.

I joined in his laughter and reached across the table and put my hand on his. "I guess we can just move on as usual."

"I sure hope so. I would hate to lose our friendship."

An hour later, sitting alone in my room, I felt confident that things would drift on like usual and that life would somehow become easier. But, I soon found out, as I started to grapple with repressed emotions, I was fooling myself.

Chapter Ten

When I was a kid, the smell of the grass sent a jolt of energy through my body as I tightened the laces on my cleats, buckled the chin strap on my helmet, or stuffed my left hand into my glove and trotted out to left field. I was always on some kind of field. I have vivid memories of the crack of the bat when I hit my first home run in Little League. I rounded the bases—smile on my face—on top of the world. I remember feeling the ball leave my hand and watching it soar thirty yards to the corner of the end zone, my best friend, Billy Fredricks, number eighty-two, diving for the winning touchdown that led us to the state playoffs.

I started thinking back on my childhood, searching for signs I may have missed. So many of my favorite memories were sports-related. But, by the time I threw that pass my senior year in high school, I knew I was different. So I started searching the far reaches of my mind for clues that pointed to my desires as a young boy.

For some reason, instead of giving me peace of mind, my conversation with Kelly brought me deeper into self-reflection— and one night, as I lay in bed, a memory popped up that I had not remembered for a long time.

One morning, before school started, I noticed a boy being

picked on a few yards away. Two other boys knocked him down, scattering his books and backpack on the ground. As they took off, I walked over, took his hand, and helped him up. His chocolate-colored skin contrasted my Scandinavian pallor, yet that had no visible effect on me. Our eyes met. I smiled a shy greeting, picked his backpack up off the ground, handed it to him, and walked off. To me, the gesture was nothing new. I was taught from a young age to help whenever possible. But for him, it was everything. The boys who knocked him down ran to the other end of the playground, laughing. I, on the other hand, was drawn near, by compassion, and unknowingly, I learned later, didn't just extend a hand, I extended hope. I also learned later that I had always been drawn closer. I loved to observe. I loved to study. I loved to experience the differences in color and texture. I would spend hours under my bed or on the top bunk engaged in imaginative play. I was drawn to differences. I was drawn to emotion. I was drawn to new experiences. The more I experienced, the more alive I felt.

I caught frogs. I chased grasshoppers. I soaked up every experience. The more I opened my mind, the happier and more fulfilled I became. I wasn't aware of this as an adolescent, but as I looked back it was clear.

I would cross the street from my house to the rundown apartments and play for hours with the kids who seemed to come from all corners of the world. We would play football, ride bikes, climb trees. I would go to their homes for a glass of water or a cookie and sometimes invite them over to my house to play in my fort or go on trips with my family on weekends. I was never afraid of new experiences.

Later that day, I was in the hall between classes. I was walking from my seventh-grade math class to PE when I heard a soft voice say my name. I turned. And there he was. I can remember as clear as day, his eyes twinkled as we stood, looking at each other in silence.

"Hey," was the first thing I could think to say.

"Hey," he responded.

He stood there, curiously looking at me. I stood and wondered. About what? I don't know. And then the bell rang, and we turned to go to class. We walked away, yet I can still remember stopping and turning to see him peering back at me and my heart pounced. At the end of the day, I was standing outside the school waiting for my bus. I saw him a ways away talking to a friend. I got on my bus, sat near the back, and looked out the window just in time to see him skip up the steps, the tall glass door closing behind him. I turned and laid my head back on the cool green vinyl of the seat, closed my eyes, and saw him in my mind. I slept hard that night and when I woke up I still saw his face. I dreamt about him all night—what exactly I dreamt, I don't remember, but I do know I was with him in my dreams.

When I arrived at school I hurried in the front door and quickly scanned the halls trying to catch a glimpse of the image that was stuck in my mind. First period ran into second and then third into lunch. Each time class ended, I searched the halls— but nothing. I was starting to wonder if the whole thing was a figment of my imagination.

I walked into the cafeteria and waded through the bustling prepubescent masses. For some reason it seemed more crowded than usual, the noise echoing off the walls. I sat at my usual table, a bit deflated. I set my brown paper bag on the table and pulled out my sandwich. I looked down and unwrapped my usual ham and cheese and took a bite, all the while hoping he would appear. I could hear my teeth chewing the meat inside my head. Something I hadn't noticed before.

I took the final bite of my sandwich and looked up at the clock at the far end of the room—ten minutes until lunch was over. My heart sank. I took a deep breath, reached my hand into the brown bag, and pulled out my juice box. I pulled the plastic bendy straw off with my left hand, unwrapped it, and stuck it into the small circle at the top of the box. I put my lips around the end of the straw and sipped. At the time it all felt like a hopeless endeavor. But as the cool liquid ran down my throat, I became acutely aware of a presence sitting next to me.

I blinked my eyes twice and nervously looked beside me. And there he was. A smile on his face.

"Hey," was the first thing I could think to say.

"Hey," he responded.

And that was it. We were inseparable for the next three years—until he moved away right at the end of our freshman year.

I never realized it before that night, lying in bed looking deep into long-forgotten memories. Unbeknownst to me, I may have had a boyfriend from seventh through ninth grade. It was unspoken, but the signs were there. I can still remember my heart beating when I called him on the phone at night. I can remember going to movies, laughing, sharing a large pop and a popcorn. He was a great friend, but he was more than that— and I mourned him after he left. I was sad for weeks. I didn't just lose a friend. I lost a part of me and now I know why.

I fell asleep that night not quite sure if I had found clarity or even if I needed any. I just knew that my feelings had probably been there forever. I woke up the next morning more awake than usual. Clarity or not, at least I was getting to know myself better.

Chapter Eleven

I worked my way through the semester. I still sat next to Kelly in psych class, but even though we enjoyed good conversation when we were together, we slowly drifted apart. Our daily coffee and chat turned into every other day and then once a week and as the weather warmed and spring was approaching summer, my life took an abrupt turn. I was sitting outside the library when my phone tickled my back pocket. I pulled it out and looked at the name on the screen. A warmth radiated through my body. I clicked the green button and put it to my ear. "Hey, sis."

A slight pause ensued and she cleared her throat. "Hey, how's it going?" Her voice was quiet and strained.

"Well," I said quizzically, trying to decipher her tone. "I'm doing good." I could feel my brows furrow. "What's going on with you? Everything okay?"

"I'm calling about Dad." The phone went silent again. I could hear what I thought were muffled tears.

"What about Dad?" I said softly.

She sobbed quietly for a moment. "He's gone."

I let her words sink in and then emitted the only thing I could think of, knowing it would sound cold, but unable to help myself, "Hmmm—Oh."

"He never woke up this morning."

"So, he went in his sleep," I replied matter-of-factly, a slight feeling of relief filling my chest.

"Yup, Mom found him when she brought him his morning coffee."

I raised my face toward the sky and let the sun warm my skin. I took a deep breath. I knew what my immediate feelings were, but wondered if I should keep them hidden. Wow—hidden again—because of my dad. It was ironic. I hid my feelings my entire life because of him. And now, when I was feeling relief, when I was feeling liberated from a father who had betrayed and disowned me, I felt like I had to stifle my truth once again. "How's mom doing?" I finally asked.

"Umm—not good. Dad's been a burden." She took a deep breath. "Who knows how she's going to recover from this."

I let out an audible sigh. "Are there any plans?"

"I'm not sure yet. Just thought I would call yuh first. Mom doesn't have the energy to call anyone."

"Oh—thanks—You gonna be alright?"

"I think so."

"Where are you now?"

"I'm sitting on the patio at Mom's."

"You plan on staying with her?"

"Probably the next few days, but who knows?"

"Take care of yourself."

"I will—It would be nice to see you. You think you can come by?" I didn't answer. "I miss you," her voice created a slight tug on my heart.

"I miss you too," I said quietly.

We sat silently for a minute before officially ending the conversation. When I hung up the phone, I sat and watched people passing by, going in and out of the pub and library. A strange mixture of happiness and anxiety mingled in my stomach. I felt an invisible weight being lifted off my shoulders, yet a lifetime of memories came rushing back. I pictured my mom sitting on the edge of the couch in the living room, head bent, crying, my sister sitting next to her, whispering consoling words. My heart beat slowly, but deliberately, as I processed the news.

Chapter Twelve

I woke to a strange feeling. The smells, the sounds—once familiar—felt like a dream. I didn't think I would ever be back at my childhood home again, especially after my last visit. I sat up in bed. My old room was now a makeshift office and guest room. The bed was pushed in the corner. A computer and lamp sat on a small desk on the other side of the room. I swung my feet over the edge of the bed, stretched my arms toward the ceiling, and yawned. A sliver of light danced through a crack in the curtains and landed on the wall at the foot of the bed.

I stood up, walked over, and pushed the curtains to the other side of the window. Light flooded the room. I looked out from my second-story perch at the deserted cul-de-sac below. Green lawns and manicured shrubs rounded the neighborhood. I shook my head and smirked. I pictured myself riding bikes and shooting hoops with my friends in their driveway across the street. It was a far cry from the life I lived just a couple years ago— waking up to cars driving by, searching for scraps of food in the nearest dumpster.

I closed my eyes and took a deep breath. "That's not my life anymore," I said to myself. I felt the sun through the window and slowly opened my eyes. This was going to be a long day. I readied myself, pulling on the dress pants and shiny shoes I bought just twenty-four hours ago. I finished buttoning the newly purchased white shirt that felt foreign to me, as I hadn't dressed up since prom my senior year of high school.

I walked to the bathroom, looked in the mirror, and cocked my head as I evaluated myself quizzically, my blue and green striped tie hanging, untied, on either side of my neck. I still remembered how to tie a tie. In fact, I still remembered when my dad took me to get my first suit in middle school. The old guy came out from behind the counter and showed me what he called a Windsor knot, explaining that it was the most elegant way to tie a man's tie. For a while, I liked to dress up every Sunday when we went to church. I felt grown up—I felt like a man —until church lost its luster. I pondered that thought for a moment and then let out an audible chuckle. "A man—isn't that ironic?" I smirked at myself in the mirror, shrugged, and then headed downstairs.

I heard the clinking of dishes and the smell of bacon coming from the kitchen, wondering if Mom was saving the crispy ends for me. "Morning," I said, as I caught a glimpse of my mom, working away at the stove.

She turned slowly, a shy grin on her face. "Good morning, sweetheart. Breakfast is almost ready."

I took a seat at the counter. "Where's sis?"

"She ran out to get coffee."

I sat in silence for a few minutes, watching the steam rise from the stove, above mom's head, and get sucked into the exhaust fan. I felt a softness rub at my ankle and leaned down and picked up the orange furball I had known so well growing up. But now, this furball was looking a little ragged. "So, how old is Sunshine now?" I asked, breaking the silence.

Mom walked to the cupboard beside the fridge and grabbed

three plates. "Oh, maybe thirteen. He's on the last of his nine lives." I chuckled as I held him tight to my chest and ran my hand over his head.

The door opened in the distance and my sister made her way into the kitchen. "You finally up, sleepyhead," she said, trying to inject life into the room.

"Halfway," I smiled in return.

The awkwardness was palpable as she set the coffees down and found a seat next to me. Mom set three plates of food between us. We ate, the clinking of cutlery the only thing keeping us company.

Soon, we found ourselves stuffed into Dad's old Ford truck, me at the helm leading our family to the memorial service at the church I hadn't stepped foot in for years. The parking lot was dotted with a few cars, as the service was still forty-five minutes away. Mom wanted to be early to make sure everything was in place. I wanted to get this over with so that they could put him in the ground and I could put him behind me.

I sat quietly in the front pew, the cold, hardwood adding to the already unpleasant feelings running through my body. I wasn't sure if the sanctuary was actually cold or if it was just being back in the dusty old church, but goosebumps formed on my arms and legs and a slight shiver ran up my spine. I looked toward the pulpit, my mom and sister were whispering back and forth as if they were hatching some elaborate scheme. Mom turned to the reverend who was standing a few feet from her. "Yeah, that will work just fine," she said to him, her voice reverberating off the brick walls.

My sister made a sudden beeline toward me. She plopped down and put her arm around my shoulders. I could tell she was struggling to keep it together. "How you doin', brother?"

She knew how I felt and was doing her best to comfort me.

I shrugged and dropped my head. "I love you sis, but I can't pretend I'm sad," I whispered. "I can't pretend I want to pay respects to the old man."

"I know—I'm sorry."

I turned and looked at her. "What do you have to be sorry about?" I paused. "You don't need to be sorry?"

"I am, though. I don't know the whole story, but I know that you had it rough and Dad was an ass," she huffed. I chuckled softly and shot her a smile. Her eyes welled with tears as she continued. "I lost you for a couple years. I didn't know where you went or what you were doing until you finally called me when you were back in school."

"Yeah, everything was messed up." I checked my phone—twenty minutes until the service. I looked around. Only a few people had arrived, scattered throughout the sanctuary, sitting quietly. "Let's go outside for a few minutes—get some fresh air before things get going."

We found our old hangout by the swings behind the Sunday school building. We sat quietly for a moment, swaying in the warm summer breeze on the two swings that seemed to have shrunk since the last time we were there.

"Well—" I looked at my sister, smiled, and then shared my story, starting with getting kicked out of school because mom and dad wouldn't sign the student loan papers. I told her about my life on the streets, eating in dumpsters and at the mission, my time at Christopher House, and how I worked my way back into college. She cried.

I knelt in front of her and put my arms around her waist. Tears ran down her face. I took a deep breath and controlled the tremble rising in my throat. "Hey—" I leaned back and looked at her. "Don't worry too much. I finally got my first kiss with a guy."

She sniffled. "How was it?"

"Uh-mazing." We both laughed.

I took her hand and we walked back toward the sanctuary. There were a few more cars in the parking lot, but it wasn't busting at the seams by any means.

As we approached the entrance, I noticed a familiar figure hanging out by the front door. I shook my head. "What you doin' here?" I called out, a smile beaming from my face.

"I had to come see you, man?" We embraced.

"I'm glad you did." I turned and put my arm around his shoulder. "Sis, you remember DJ, don't you?"

"Of course. I still remember you guys riding bikes off those old ramps you used to build in the cul-de-sac."

"Bahah—" We laughed in unison.

We walked inside and found our seats. A short, uncomfortable affair ensued. We hugged and shook hands with people we hadn't seen in some time. I bit my tongue and smiled cordially as we ate refreshments afterward, nodding thanks to those who offered us prayers. Once we got home, I left as quickly as I could. I said goodbye to Mom, who offered little comfort and then my sister drove me to the bus station. We shared a long hug and a few more tears.

"I'll keep in touch, sis."

"You better." She grabbed my hand and squeezed it tightly.

* * *

That night I sat at the small desk in my room near campus, replaying the conversation with my sister. I thought about how I described the cold nights on the street as I slept in the alleyway downtown. And I relived her tears. I thought about sharing the story of my first kiss and I heard her quiet laughter. I had tried to separate myself from my past life, the life before everything fell apart. I had tried to move on—and thought that I had. But it was apparent that was not the case. The memories—good and bad—were still there. So, I opened my laptop and pulled up the college website. I clicked on the little magnifying glass in the top left corner of the screen and typed, "counseling department," and scrolled through the results. About halfway down the page a heading, *Student Services,* caught my attention. I found the counseling resources—academic and career guidance, social/emotional support, and mental health counseling. I ruled out academic and career, but read through the social/emotional and then mental health descriptions. I sat back in my chair and put my hands behind my head. I closed my eyes and thought for a moment. I was nervous and, once again, a knot formed in my belly.

I leaned forward, placed my hand on my laptop, moving the cursor and hovering over the social/emotional link. I stared at the highlighted words for a moment and then navigated my way through. A few minutes later I had a confirmed appointment with a social worker sitting in my inbox. And three days later I found myself sitting in a small waiting room, holding an old magazine that I had taken from a side table next to the stiff-backed chair I had chosen to sit in.

I thumbed through the magazine aimlessly, looking at the well-worn pages. I wasn't even sure what I was looking at. I was nervous, my mind elsewhere. I had never been to counseling before. I didn't know what to expect. I looked up at the clock on the wall. Time seemed to be speeding up—my appointment quickly approaching.

I felt my heart pound. I didn't know why I couldn't relax. I made the appointment. No one forced me to be there, yet I felt trapped. I felt stuck between what I wanted to keep to myself and what I would be asked to share with a total stranger. I closed my eyes and laid my head back on the wall behind me. I suddenly traveled in time, back to the one time I was sent to the principal's office in middle school. I felt if I opened my eyes I would see Mrs. Bradley sitting behind the counter, her hair pulled tight into a bun at the top of her head. I knew I would see Scotty Moore, the troublemaker who caused me to be sitting next to him waiting for the principal to dole out punishment. Finally, I heard my name called. I slowly opened my eyes. No Mrs. Bradley. No Scotty Moore.

The secretary directed me down the hall. I walked a ways down, looking at the intermittent artwork on the walls, to an open door on the left. I stepped inside. A man, about forty, stood up and greeted me with a soft smile. He introduced himself and motioned to a well-used, brown, leather chair. I sat.

"So, nice to meet you," He said as he flipped through a red spiral notepad. "How are you doing today?"

"Good—for the most part. But, a bit nervous to be honest."

"That's natural. Do you know what you're nervous about?"

"I'm not quite sure. I guess I don't know how ready I am to share."

"Okay. Can you tell me what it is you're thinking about sharing?" I took a deep breath. "Take your time," he said reassuringly.

I put my hands together, interlacing my fingers, and brought them toward my face. My thumbs rested on my lips as I took a moment to think.

"If it would make you feel better," the doctor said in a relaxed tone. "I can get us started."

"Yeah, okay."

"On the form you filled out when you made the appointment, you wrote a couple general things you wanted to talk about. The first was your parents... and the second was some personal issues."

I raised my eyebrows and nodded.

"Do you have a preference where we start?'

"That's just it," I said. "I can't separate one from the other."

"Can you tell me what you mean by that?"

"Well, I think my personal issues come from issues I have with my parents."

"I get that," he said with a thoughtful look on his face. He jotted down a couple notes. "Can you start off by telling me one of the issues?" He leaned back a bit in his chair and squinted his eyes. "Maybe the one that is foremost in your mind?" He sat patiently.

"I guess the biggest thing is, I was homeless for almost a year. In fact, I lived on the street."

He nodded his head slowly. "Can you tell me when that was?"

"Just a couple of years ago. I was enrolled here at the college and then my life was turned upside down and one day I woke up in the alley downtown."

"That sounds serious."

"Yeah. I thought I had put it behind me, but that and a few other things keep creeping into my life."

"Understandable. It's tough to move on from difficult times, even if you're no longer in the same situation."

I smiled and started feeling a bit more comfortable.

We talked for another forty-five minutes until the hour was up. I opened up about my most painful experiences. It felt like going backward, but it also felt necessary, it also felt— freeing. I shared my parents' religious background. I shared how they disowned me after I told them I was gay and how that ended my student loans and how I couch-surfed for a bit before finding myself eating out of dumpsters and at the local Gospel mission. By the time we were done, my nerves were gone and I was looking forward to my next appointment.

Twenty minutes later I found myself daydreaming, sipping coffee a block away from the counseling office, thinking about what I would share next week when I felt a hand on my shoulder.

I looked up. "Jeff?" I was caught off guard.

"Hey." He paused briefly. "How's it going?"

"Okay," I said, a quizzical look on my face.

"It's been a while," he replied with a half-smile.

"Yeah, it has." I shook my head. "Last time, I remember you were sitting in the quad with Tim and Joey—and when I got there you got up and left." I didn't want to mention seeing him outside the club that night—and it seemed he was glad I didn't mention it, as well.

"That's about right." He nodded. "You mind if I sit?"

"No—uh—yeah—take a seat," I stammered. "What you been up to?"

"Just trying to get through classes right now." He tried to act relaxed as he pulled out a chair and sat down. "What about you?"

"Dealing with my shit—" I laughed. *Here I go again, sharing what I didn't want to share.*

"Oh—really?" He raised his eyebrows.

"I just got out of a counseling session."

78

"You always seem so together."

"Thought I had things together, too—until I realized I didn't."

"I went to counseling for a couple years when I was in high school." He nodded his head. "Got me through some rough years," he said with a sideways smile.

We sat there quietly for a moment. I pursed my lips and tilted my head to the right, trying to get up the courage to say my next statement. "I think I've gotten through the toughest part—at least I'm hoping I have."

"Whaddya mean?"

"I went through some trauma a few years back. I thought I put it behind me, but it feels like some of it is just hanging in the background. I mean, the effects are still causing me a bit of confusion."

"It's good you're dealing with it."

"I was nervous going in."

"Sure, I was too. How do you feel now?"

"Better. I think I can go back in next week more confident."

"That's good."

"So, anyway, what you doing here?" I looked at him, a little puzzled. "You're not drinking coffee I see."

"I was here with a study group from my econ class. I saw you come in just as we were leaving and I wanted to say hi."

"Oh—I'm glad you did."

We sat there for a few more minutes meandering through conversation—talking about nothing in particular—both seeming to avoid the night at the club that revealed maybe a little more than Jeff was hoping—whether consciously or unconsciously, I'm not sure.

The conversation slowed. We sat quietly for a while and then simultaneously got up and awkwardly walked out together. We said goodbye and headed in our separate directions.

"Hey," Jeff's voice popped out of nowhere. I turned. Halfway across the parking lot, he took a couple steps toward me. "I borrowed my dad's motorcycle and was gonna go for a ride in the morning. You wanna come along?"

I let out a muffled chuckle and raised my eyebrows. I stumbled over my words. "Uh—well—I don't have any plans."

"Pick you up at nine?"

"I should of had my coffee by then," I replied, trying to muster some enthusiasm.

"Great. See you in the morning." We raised our hands at each other.

I walked off and shook my head slightly, a bit perplexed—but also a bit intrigued.

* * *

The next morning I woke with a few small butterflies floating around in my stomach. I wasn't sure what to feel as I got up and readied myself for a morning on the back of Jeff's bike. I thought I would let the day ramble on as it would and not worry about anything, but I couldn't help but try to unscramble what I felt was a bit of a riddle emerging in front of me. I wasn't sure what to think of this new side of Jeff. His coldness toward me over the past year was a heavy contrast to an invitation to ride pillion on a morning jaunt to who knows where. I sat at the small round table squeezed between the fading leather couch I found at the thrift store down the street and the tiny kitchen that took up half the square footage of my one-room studio.

I took a deep breath and thought back to the first night we met, the night the four of us went to the bar, the same night I met Kelly. "Hmmm..." I said to no one. I remembered Jeff's smile across the table just off the dance floor. I didn't really remember noticing it back then, but I recalled we were all in a good mood. He leaned over to me a couple of times in conversation over the music and put his hand on mine and then I caught a glimpse of Kelly, leaning against the wall by the speaker. My heart pounded softly.

I turned back toward Jeff in my mind and then back toward Kelly. I juxtaposed the two of them in that environment—the music blaring—my quick draw away from Jeff and toward the new guy across the room. I pictured myself walking toward Kelly and imagined Jeff watching me approach this stranger. I told myself I was probably making more of it than there was, but couldn't help but wonder.

I sipped the last of my coffee, stood up, and walked into the kitchen. I turned on the faucet with a soft squeak, filled the cup until it overflowed, and then dumped it out and set the cup upside down in the sink. I glanced at the watch on my left wrist. It was almost nine. I walked to the one small closet next to the front door and grabbed a jacket and my small backpack and soon found myself sitting on the front steps, a soft wind mingling with the warming sun, when I heard a deep rumble approaching. I glanced down the road and noticed what I figured was Jeff, riding up smoothly to the curb. The bike idled, purring a deep baritone, as Jeff sat there and pulled the black helmet from his head. "Hey, you ready for a ride," he hollered over the rumble. I stood up, raised my right hand in greeting, and met him at the curb. He handed me a helmet and told me to hop on. I pulled the helmet over my head, tightened the chin strap, and jumped on the back.

"You can grab the handles on either side of the seat or you can grab my waist," he said as he turned and looked at me over his shoulder. A bit uncomfortable, I grabbed the handles and wiggled my rear end around until I felt a little more secure. And then, with a small jolt, we were off.

We whizzed through crowded streets, cars parked on either side, people walking up and down the sidewalks. We slowed down at a stop sign and then sped around the corner with a whirl. We leaned to the right and I lost my nerve, quickly letting go of the handles and wrapping my arms around Jeff's midsection.

"You okay," he blared over the vibrating thunder that enveloped our entire bodies.

"Oh yeah, just trying to hold on," I replied, a bit sarcastically, eyes closed.

"I'm gonna hit the freeway here in a minute. You think you can handle it?"

"Won't know unless we try," I said with a bit of trepidation.

"Just hold on tight. We'll be just fine."

We slowed down as we made our way around a corner and then up a hill toward the on ramp. The vibrato of the bike switched to a leisurely hum as we climbed the hill and took a slight turn toward the freeway. A sudden downshift and the hum turned to a swarm of bees as we picked up speed, merged, and became one with the river of vehicles headed south down the interstate.

The wind whistled through my helmet. The stationary objects on the side of the freeway blurred to bodyless colors of grays and browns and soon, I felt comfortable. I started to relax and my grip on Jeff's midsection loosened. Time seemed to pass quickly as the sun danced through the trees on the east side of the freeway and the intermittent overpasses threw quick patches of shade on the ground as we sped by. We exited to the right, down a slight decline, around a corner, and then up a ramp that took us onto a bridge that connected the city to the west and to saltwater beaches.

We rode for a few more minutes, making our way across the bridge, and weaved through close-knit neighborhoods packed with cars and people. I recognized where we were as I had come here a few times with my family. We pulled into a parking lot adjacent to a large park. Flashbacks of family outings with picnic baskets and blankets woke the butterflies in my stomach as we parked near the entrance, dismounted, and removed our helmets.

"So, how was the ride?" Jeff asked with a smile on his face.

"I enjoyed it," I said, turning my head and looking around, not quite comfortable making direct eye contact.

"You wanna walk around the park for a while? There's some trails that lead to the beach."

"Sure. That'd be nice."

We walked through the park, passed a group playing disc golf, and then found what appeared to be a church group getting ready to play softball a little ways away. We sat on a bench and watched as they organized their teams. We made small talk—twisting our way through topics with no real depth, both struggling to find something comfortable to land on. We blew through our favorite foods, we mentioned movies we'd seen, our favorite music, but nothing stuck. There were awkward pauses between one topic and the next. We sat quietly and watched the teams as they took their place on the field and the first batter walked out of the dugout.

"Swing and a miss," Jeff called out as the first batter whiffed at the ball. We both laughed. "Ooh," he said with excitement.

"He got a piece of it that time," he added as the ball flew off the bat, but landed foul.

We spent the next fifteen minutes commentating— "Safe on first," I called out as one batter barely out-touched the throw to the bag. "A comedy of errors, right through the shortstop's legs," I completed my diatribe. We watched as the next batter hit a high flyball, the center fielder took a few quick steps back and made a heroic catch over his right shoulder.

Our play-by-play slowed, and then halted, and then bumped along a bit more as we sat and watched the game continue. "Okay," Jeff said, trying to transition our rutty conversation to something more pleasant. "You wanna walk toward the beach."

"Yeah, why not." I inadvertently reached out and put my hand on his left leg as we both turned and our eyes met. I quickly realized what I had done and, gave him a quick smile and stood up.

We walked lazily through the trees and found the path that overlooked the water. We meandered in silence, in no rush to talk or to arrive at our destination. The canopy of trees kept us in semi-darkness as we looked out upon the rocky shoreline below. The water lapped up against the edge of the beach, moving out a little farther with each deviation of the tide. The path began its descent and the trees opened up. The sun beat down its pre-afternoon rays, working hard to warm our bodies as it covered us with light, yet it was still a couple hours away from full strength.

We hit the sand and headed toward the water. "You ever been here before?" Jeff asked.

"A few times with my family. We usually just stayed at the park most of the time. I try not to think about it."

"Oh, why not?"

"That's part of the reason I'm going to counseling."

"Family issues. I get it."

"And with my dad dying recently, things just floated to the surface."

"Ahh, sorry. I didn't know."

"It's okay. It was a relief. That's part of what I am working through."

"Oh, not a good relationship, huh?"

"That's an understatement."

He stopped walking and turned toward me. "What happened—if you don't mind me asking?"

I took a short breath in. "Hmph." I paused for a moment. "Not sure." I took a deeper breath and let it out slowly. "I haven't talked about it much."

"It's okay if you don't want to."

"If I was gonna say anything it would be that he was a prick."

Jeff shook his head. "Sorry, man. Didn't mean to bring it up."

"It's okay." We turned toward the water and walked in silence. "He really was a prick," I let out a muffled laugh.

Jeff put his arm around my shoulders. "If you ever want to talk, just let me know." He removed his arm, looked down at the wet sand, and then out at the water.

We watched the tide move slowly in and out, creating foam and a few scattered bubbles in its wake. We took off our shoes and socks and put them on top of a rock, rolled up our pant legs, and then waded through the edge of the water, slimy seaweed encircling our ankles as the water covered our calves and then dissipated.

We turned over barnacle-covered rocks and found small crabs and discarded shells. We pushed driftwood back to sea, we watched seagulls fly high overhead and dive to the ground in search of scraps. We said few words, as comfort became our friend.

"You getting hungry?" Jeff asked. He looked at his watch. "It's almost noon."

"I could use a bite."

"There's a few restaurants just down the road if you want."

"That sounds good. As long as I can get this sand from between my toes." I smiled.

We wiped off our feet as best we could and put our shoes on, then climbed back onto the path and retraced our steps— back under the canopy of trees—by the softball field where the two teams had retreated to food and drink on the picnic tables behind the backstop—to the now vacant disc golf course—and back to the parking lot.

We were soon mounted back on the bike and headed down the road toward restaurants and the ferry terminal. "What you feel up to?" Jeff's voice called over the din of the engine.

"Pizza, burgers, fish-n-chips, whatever."

"How 'bout this up here?" He pointed to a small pizza joint to our left.

"Sure. Go for it."

We pulled in, found a seat in a booth amongst the few scattered patrons, and ordered a large meat eaters special. Sitting across from each other in the quiet brought back the small awkward pauses. Fortunately, the pizza came quickly and we had something to stuff in our mouths and we also had something more to talk about.

"Ooh, man, this is good." I blurted out, mouth full of cheesy meat.

"This reminds me of the time I microwaved a couple frozen

pizzas back in high school and woke up the next morning with heartburn," his retort muffled by the cheese filling his mouth and stretching from his lips to the slice in his hand.

I laughed. "So, you caught my sarcasm."

"It was either that or your taste buds are broken." We laughed in unison, but continued filling our bellies, and the awkward pauses seemed to melt away.

"You have any plans tonight?" Jeff asked.

"I was going to work on a paper."

"You wanna skip that and catch the ferry?"

"Doesn't take much for me to put off writing a term paper."

"Great—the terminal's just down the road."

Soon, we were headed down the long winding hill toward the end of the line of cars waiting to make their way onto the ferry. The right side of the road was packed with small homes on the water's edge—tiny to no yards with little to no parking, with a view only millionaires could afford.

The bike purred as we patiently made our stop-and-go approach to the small ticket booth at the front of the line. The sun was close to its high point in the sky. My still body warmed and I could feel a small drop of sweat following the ridges of my spine and finding a stopping point at the crook of my lower back.

I flipped up the shield on my helmet and looked up. Long white streaks of clouds softly contrasted with the arctic blue of the sun-drenched sky. A lone airplane looked as if it was suspended in place above us. I looked to my right, over to the houses packed on the side of the road overlooking the waters. I imagined myself knocking on one of the doors and joining friends on the back deck for a barbecue. We sat and talked, admiring the view as we watched kids flying kites with their parents on the beach below. We ate burgers—talked about our classes—walked down the long stairs that led to the beach and skipped rocks into the rippling water.

I was jolted back to reality as the bike revved and propelled us forward. We turned right and drove until the ticket booth came into view. After buying our tickets, we joined another line, waiting for the current ferrygoers to unload. Pedestrians filed out. Cars, trucks, and vans slowly made their way from the ferry to the road, passed us, and then up the hill and out of sight toward their destinations.

The barricade arm lifted and we made our way onto the vehicle deck. It was packed from end to end—we were jammed in the middle between a small yellow school bus and a brand-new Mercedes, temporary license plate taped to the inside of the rear window. We removed our helmets and took the stairs to the seating area. We wound our way through rows of seats, walked outside to the front of the viewing deck, and found a spot on the railing. I leaned forward and allowed the wind to cool my face. Standing with my eyes shut, I could feel Jeff's body close to mine. He gently wrapped his arm around my waist. Although I was enjoying the day, I wasn't sure what to think. Questions still lingered about what was going on between us. I took a deep breath, and let the pungent salt air fill my nose and lungs.

He took a breath. "Can't get better than this," he said as he let it out.

I stayed silent. My mind went back to the night at the bar as I approached Kelly. I could not help seeing Jeff watching me walk away from him and toward the stranger dancing against the wall. I nodded my head and added, "The wind feels good," trying to sound authentic.

"Sorry about that," Jeff said, removing his arm from my waist. He turned and smiled. I glanced at him out of the corner of my eye and shrugged. "You okay?" he added.

"Yeah, I'm having a good time. That's not it—just not sure what we're doing." We stared into the water at the approaching land mass, letting time pass and words fade off into the distance. "We're getting close. Might as well head back down," I said, trying to break the tension. I thought about grabbing his hand and leading him down the stairs, but I didn't want to give him the wrong impression, so I pulled back.

A few minutes later the ferry came to a stop and the bike purred its baritone song. I took my place behind him and fumbled with my hands between the handles and his waist, finally deciding on his waist.

The ride off the ferry and down the tree-lined road was quiet, save for the bike as it shook our bodies rhythmically. My mind wandered while we traveled farther from home. We came to a stop at a little shop on the side of the road, parked, and got off. We set our helmets on the bike and stood for a while. Jeff ran his hands through his hair and looked around.

"I'm sorry how I treated you," he said, sheepishly. "I mean, not—not today. I mean—before this. Since the night at the bar when I dropped you off." I looked at him. He was looking off into the distance. "I didn't know it at the time. That's no excuse, but I didn't know at the time. I think—I think I was jealous." I raised my eyebrows and nodded. He stammered a bit—tried to say a few more words, but went silent.

This time I took his hand gently and led him to a bench in front of the store. I let go of his hand as we sat. We looked at each other and then looked away.

"You want a root beer?" I said, feeling the gesture would

lighten the mood.

He took a shallow breath and nodded.

I emerged from the store with a cold can in each hand. I sat next to him and handed him his drink.

We opened the cans simultaneously—*Pop-Pop*—the bubbles wafted through the air. We sipped slowly, enjoying the sweetness—enjoying the suds as they tickled our noses.

We sat on the bench, in the outdoors, something that was once home to me, a place, the only place for almost a year, I called my home, and for some reason, I was drawn back to my time on the street. I pictured myself sitting on the bench on the side of the road after I left the morning meal at the mission. I had just talked to Pastor Jim and was contemplating my next move. I could still remember his comforting words. I could still remember the smell of burnt bacon. I saw myself getting up from the bench and walking the mile to what would be my salvation—my first trip to Christopher House.

I let distant images float through my mind. I felt I was remembering an early crossroads in my life and wondered why now. Why did these images, these memories I had tried to move on from, invade my thoughts at this moment? I remembered Nadine walking through the door in the waiting room and working her magic—getting me everything I needed to feel comfortable that first night—soap and a hot shower, a toothbrush and toothpaste, and a bed. She, and Jeremiah Bailey, are the reasons I was able to move on, to go back to school, to get my life back on track.

I looked off in the distance. "I get it. It's okay."

"Thanks. It's bothered me for a while."

We didn't say anything more and soon were on the ferry again, headed toward the mainland, toward the road home. It was a quiet ride back—not many words exchanged. However, this time, the silence was welcomed. There was a comfort in the wind blowing through our bodies as we made our way off the ferry, up and through the curvy road past the park, and then back onto the freeway. The bike came to a stop in front of my apartment. The engine sputtered and went silent. I got off and handed the helmet to Jeff. He took his off and held it under his arm. He looked at me and smiled. "Thanks for the day."

I smiled back. "Sure, thanks for inviting me." We paused for a moment and then I stuck out my hand. We shook, both making sure not to hold on too long. I turned and held up my hand in the air as I walked away.

Chapter Thirteen

I was quietly sitting in the waiting room of the counseling office with my eyes closed, head leaning back on the wall. This time I stayed in the present—no time traveling—and I was getting more comfortable with each visit. During my second session, I talked about my day spent with Jeff and my inevitable confusion. Last week, I talked about my father's death and about the last words he said to me, "Don't call." I told the doctor I felt relief when my sister told me he was gone and that I didn't feel bad about it. Then again, that was also a bit confusing. But he reassured me that my feelings were okay. He said that I had the right to feel that way because it was my truth.

I sat there and ran through the mysteries of my life, trying to figure out what new nugget I would share with my counselor and inevitably admit to myself. An hour later I emerged from the session with, if not clarity, at least a new realization. I must have repressed an awful lot of feelings because until I opened up in that twelve-by-twelve, one-windowed office, I only had a few cursory thoughts about Jeff. Now the question was eating at me, "What the fuck is up with him?" I walked down the hall, out of the waiting room, and into the summer's day.

As I walked across campus, I realized I had moved from the counseling building to the library without realizing where I was going. Lost in thought, I turned and headed to the coffee cart across the way. I grabbed a bagel and an Italian soda and filled my belly while I tried to clear my head—while I tried to refocus on the research paper I had to work on. I spent a few minutes watching students go this way and that, in and out of the pub on one side and the library on the other. I saw a few familiar faces, nodded to a professor I hadn't seen since freshman year, washed down the last bite of bagel, and then made my way to the top floor of the library where I had made my second home for the last three years.

My usual cubicle was occupied, so I sat in a stall across the aisle. I pulled out my laptop and two library books I had previously checked out on social services in the inner city. I looked through sticky notes, filled with chicken scratch, that marked a dozen or so pages and then thumbed through a black and white composition book. I stopped at a list of research topics, half of which were scratched out, a few with asterisks, and a single phrase circled three times—"Hemorrhaging Social Service Agencies and the Homeless Epidemic." *Another light day of reading and research*, I scoffed to myself.

I spent the next two hours reading and rereading my notes—rereading, highlighting, and annotating passages in the books I had chosen. I was intrigued, yet, at the same time, I was lost. I was struggling to narrow down my focus. My main claim was that the state government is not adequately addressing the increasing homeless population in the city while allocating hundreds of millions of dollars to projects that benefit people who have means. I had thirty pages to fill, and, at first, I thought I wouldn't be able to find enough information—but I quickly realized I had too much.

I started thinking about my personal experiences—living

on the streets, sleeping in an alleyway that was crowded from end to end with tents and makeshift abodes with people who had been there a month, a few months, a few years— overhearing staff at the mission talk about dwindling resources and hoping they had enough food to reach the end of a line that got longer each day—and working at Christopher House, that received scanty government funding and was only able to survive because of the generosity of community donations. In fact, the computer I used to apply for college along with a half dozen others sitting on tables in a tiny room at the back of Christopher House, and one old, barely adequate printer, was donated by a family who was closing down their tech store a few blocks away.

I flipped through the sticky notes in one of the books until I found a chapter called, "Lack of Funding Leads to Closed Doors," read through a few paragraphs I had previously marked, and made up my mind. I would use a combination of research, personal experience, and interviews, to complete my paper. I could easily finish it sitting in the library, but I was compelled to do more. I finally realized that I had to live with what I once tried to forget. And, in order to do so, I had to come to terms with it. I had to revisit, to embrace, to work at understanding how this time in my life influenced me moving forward.

I turned to my laptop and sent an email to my professor explaining my idea and asking for a week's extension. That would give me a month to complete the paper. I then sent an email to Nadine at Christopher House. Two days later, I had the okay from my professor and a meeting set up with Nadine. Now, to make it all come together, I needed to find a ride to Christopher House, the Mission, and my old home in the alley. I needed to find someone to accompany me on my journey and to help me deal with the inevitable emotions that would resurface.

I mulled over my options. I picked up my phone and scrolled through my contact list until I came to Kelly's name. I hadn't talked to him for over a month, but I was compelled to call him since, other than my sister and counselor, he was really the only one I had talked to about my time on the street. I clicked on his number and tapped the little green phone icon at the bottom of the screen. It rang three times. My heartbeat quickened.

"Hello," a familiar voice answered.

I paused briefly. "Hey."

"Man, it's been a while. What you up to?"

"I was calling to see if you were in town."

"I'm visiting my parents for the summer. I won't be home for another few weeks."

"Ah, I see."

"Why? What's up?"

I explained the idea for my paper and told him I was hoping he would be able to go with me during my interviews, especially my visit to my old home in the alley downtown.

"Oh—I wish I could."

"I haven't told anyone else about living on the street, besides my sister and counselor. Anyway, I'll figure it out."

"It sounds like a great idea, for both your term paper and maybe even for your own growth. I'd love to read it when you're done"

"Yeah, sure—I'd love to have you read it."

We talked for a few more minutes. He asked me about counseling—and then I asked him about getting coffee when he returned to campus—and then I turned back to my contact list and scrolled up and down. I could call my sister, but I really didn't want her to see where I lived while I was missing from her life. A few other names caught my attention, but I couldn't find the courage to share my history with them.

I gathered my stuff and headed back to my apartment. I got home, laid on my bed, and set my phone on my chest. I closed my eyes and felt rhythmic breaths going in and out. Names danced in my head, but I shooed them all away, except one, that kept popping up. I took a couple easy breaths trying to muster the courage to make the call—and finally picked up the phone. It rang—

"Hello?"

"Hello—Jeff?"

Chapter Fourteen

Jeff rolled up in his car as I sat on the stoop in front of my apartment wondering how he would react when I gave him a more detailed account of the upcoming day. It was just eight o'clock and my meeting with Nadine was set for ten, so we stopped at a coffee shop and got a bite to eat. I ordered a black coffee and a bagel. Jeff ordered a latte and a breakfast sandwich. We sat in the corner at a small round table. The bustle of people and the soft music in the background were comforting.

We relaxed for a bit, sipping and pecking away at our food, and finally, Jeff broke the silence. "So, I'm curious—" He paused.

"About?" I lifted my head and looked at him.

"—why you decided to call me?"

I shrugged. "Thought I would return the favor."

"Ah—I see—repaying me for the day on the town." He looked content.

I smiled awkwardly and shook my head. "Not exactly—for the ambiguity." I looked down at my bagel and then back at Jeff who was looking a little askew, trying to figure out my meaning. "I'm still not quite sure why you asked me on the bike ride. I mean—I have my inklings, but nothing substantial." We looked at each other for a moment and then he nodded slightly. "We haven't had the best interactions since we've met," I continued, hoping for some clarity, but added, "In fact, I'd say they were a bit confusing."

"Yeah—true. He nodded again. "I can see why you're confused." He looked around, took a sip of his latte, and then leaned back in his chair, furrowing his brows and folding his arms.

"I think I can figure it out, but thought spending a bit more time together would help." We shared a shy laugh. "I also have a few things I want to let you know about my appointment today." He raised his eyebrows. "I told you about my paper." He nodded knowingly. "There's a bit more to it." He squinted in anticipation. "Well—" I took a breath. "Well—I was homeless for almost a year." I leaned forward and put my forearms on the table. "When I told my mom and dad I was gay, they kicked me out of the house—unofficially kicked me out—but it was pretty clear what they wanted." He sat there listening diligently. I cleared my throat to allow myself a second to muster up a bit more courage. "It wasn't until a few weeks into my freshman year that I even knew they disowned me. I received a letter from the registrar that my student loans were not coming through. And then, with a bit of research, I found out that my parents decided not to sign the FAFSA papers without telling me. I lost my loan, was dropped from my classes, and had to leave the dorm."

"Shit," he said under his breath.

I chuckled awkwardly. "I spent some time sleeping on friends' couches, but that wore out quickly." We sat quietly, letting the gravity of the topic linger and sink in. "One day I snuck into my parents' house and took some camping supplies—a tent and a sleeping bag, a little gas stove, and a few other things—and then looked for a place to sleep."

"Fuck, man, that's rough," he reacted with visible emotion.

"It took me two weeks to find my permanent campsite. I was kicked out of a couple parks and a dirt patch next to the river."

"Oh." He shook his head.

"So, other than needing a ride," I chuckled, " I really need someone with me when I revisit my old home—my home on the street."

"For sure—yeah—I understand." I could tell he was looking for words to be supportive.

"So, our first stop is Christopher House. It's the place that got me off the street. I have a ten o'clock appointment to interview a lady named Nadine. She was my first contact there." I looked at him, trying to get a feel for what he was thinking. "And then, if you're up to it, we'll take a walk through the alley where I lived."

"Oh." He pursed his lips and raised his eyebrows. "Yeah—we can do that."

"I want to see if a couple people are willing to talk, but we have to catch them at the right time. I have a few questions I've put together for my research. We either need to go there about thirty minutes after dinner is over at the mission or come back one of the mornings in the next couple of days. But, I want to go there when it's still light first and just allow myself to experience it again."

"We're on your schedule. Just tell me what you need."

"I appreciate it." We sat again, sipping and finishing our food. "I'm not quite sure how I will react today—to any of it."

"Don't worry. Do what you need to do. I'll be here for whatever you need."

"You don't know how much that means to me." I shook my

head. "I think I'm ready—and I know I'll be better off once I face it head-on—but I'm anxious and knowing you will be there is a relief."

"Understandable. I'll do what I can."

A little while later we were parked two blocks from Christopher House. I opened the door and my olfactory senses were flooded with memories—the mixture of hot cement, distant salt water, and the faint hint of stale garbage made me dizzy as I was sucked back in time. I turned and placed my right foot, then my left foot on the pavement. I stood up, but lost my balance and quickly put my hands on the roof of the car to steady myself. I wasn't ready for such a visceral reaction.

Jeff rushed to my side of the car and put his hand on my shoulder. "You okay?"

"I hope so," I said, eyes closed, still holding on to the car for support.

"Take your time," he said supportively, his hand still on my shoulder.

"Man—" I shook my head. "I knew I was a bit nervous to come back, but I didn't think it would hit me this hard."

"Don't worry, it's only nine-forty. We can take it slow."

I opened my eyes and looked around, a sense of vertigo rushed over me like a strong wind. It felt like a dream. Everything was eerily familiar, and I could tell I was still grappling with a lingering emotional hangover. "Yeah, thanks. I guess I've bottled up a lot more than I thought." I turned and flashed Jeff a tense grin. There was no fooling him or myself—this was going to be a roller coaster.

My equilibrium started to stabilize as we made our way to our destination. I tried my best to take everything in as if I were a bystander, a sightseer, as if I was detached from the surroundings, but my mind and body knew differently. Everything was so familiar, yet so foreign. I had tried so hard to distance myself, to forget, yet my mind knew I had some attachment to the sights and sounds around me, while my heart was fighting to keep its distance. I could feel a tug-of-war going on inside my gut. I felt a queasiness in the pit of my stomach that began to rise. I thought I was going to throw up, but did my best to calm my nerves. I took a deep breath and worked on steadying the thumping in my chest.

Jeff reached over and took my hand as the building came into view. The sign above the door looked like it always had—big white letters, outlined in black, over a rainbow of mismatched colors. The normal clutter of tents was huddled near the entrance, a few inhabitants keeping vigil over their belongings.

We walked up to the door and as I reached for the worn brass handle it felt like I was reaching to shake the hand of an old friend. I felt a warmth rush through my body. I pressed the latch with my thumb and slowly pulled it open, revealing the same starkly decorated waiting room I became accustomed to not long ago. Unlike the first time I walked in, the friendly face I was looking for was sitting behind the desk, talking on the phone. My heart skipped a beat as she turned and her face lit up.

"I've got to go. My ten o'clock appointment just walked in." She hung up the phone and stood up. "Well, isn't that a sight for sore eyes?" she said as she turned her attention toward me.

"Hey, Nadine." I felt my face flush.

"You're sure looking good."

"Thanks. It's nice to see you."

She walked out from behind the desk, opened her arms, and wrapped them around me. I felt my body melt. It was a homecoming I never thought I would experience—one that I would never have at the home I grew up in—one that I never knew would feel so good.

She loosened her hold on me, took a step back, put her hands on my shoulders, and smiled. "I've been looking forward to this ever since you called," she said.

"Me too."

"Who's your friend?" She turned and smiled.

"This is Jeff. He was nice enough to come with me. We're gonna visit the Gospel Mission and my old home in the alley downtown. I'm pretty nervous to go back."

"That's nice of you Jeff," Nadine said. "It's good to have the support of a friend. It could be a pretty emotional visit."

Jeff smiled and thanked her and then Nadine took us on a little tour of the modest facilities before we sat down for an informal question-and-answer session.

"So, when I called, you mentioned Jeremiah doesn't work here anymore."

"Yeah, he got a job as the executive director at an inpatient treatment facility."

"That sounds like something he'd be good at." I nodded my head.

"He was the prime candidate. They actually recruited him."

"Wow, that's cool. Who took his place?"

"I think you know Pastor Jim."

"Yeah. He's the pastor from the Gospel Mission that referred me to Christopher House."

"His church has taken a big role in our programming, so we hired Pastor to take Jeremiah's place. He's only here a couple days a week right now. He still has some obligations at the mission. He's supposed to start splitting his time between here and the church at the end of the month."

"I really like Pastor Jim. He should be a good fit here."

"Yes. It's going to work out nicely."

I continued my questions, asking about funding sources, the percentage of government funding versus private funding and donations, and about specific state and federal laws regulating day-to-day operations.

She shared the organization's bylaws and the sponsoring church's guidelines that help them set goals and determine funding, staffing, and program needs. She gave me a copy of their "mission statement," *Service to the community and its people by the grace of God.* "We do not preach to those we serve," she said. "We offer small services to those who wish to attend. We give info about local church services in the area to those who ask. But, the help we provide is only contingent upon need and nothing else. Our calling is to spread God's word through service, through compassion, and through love of humanity."

I understood everything she said. I remembered the day I walked in—the day she offered her hand to me in my time of need. She served me true to her calling—true to the mission of Christopher House—and I witnessed both her and Jeremiah do the same for countless others while I was there.

I looked at my watch. It was almost noon.

"We should probably get going. I want to get to the mission during lunch so Jeff can see the action," I said.

"Yup, that's an experience we should all have at least once in our life," Nadine laughed.

We hugged one more time and she encouraged me to come back again. I told her I wanted to find a way to volunteer with homeless programs when my studies wound down.

"Thanks again—I'll see you soon," I said as Jeff and I made

our way back to the sidewalk amongst the tents outside the entrance.

We headed down the block back to the car, walking in silence, letting the last couple of hours soak in. It was a much more pleasant walk this time, now that it felt like I had acclimated to my old surroundings. Meeting with Nadine was a comfort I didn't see coming. She filled a void my parents left a long time ago.

We got in the car and sat for a moment. Jeff turned toward me and smiled. "What you feel like doing next?"

I breathed in through my nose softly. "Can we just sit here for a few minutes? I feel like I'm finally getting comfortable."

"Yeah, of course."

I leaned my head back and allowed old memories to run through my mind—walking the streets handing out socks to other homeless people—sharing stories with the other men living and working at Christopher House—remembering my final goodbyes before going back to college—all the positive things that had come into my life the last few months before I escaped the streets. I started to see how my life had shaped into what it is today. I was finally able to see my time on the streets was more than just a conglomeration of mishaps and bad circumstances.

"Well—you feel like heading toward the mission?" I finally asked. "We should be able to catch the tail end of the crowd."

"Yup. How're you feeling?"

"Much better."

"Good to hear."

By the time we reached the mission, the line was dwindling to its end. We found a parking space a block away, walked through the departing mealgoers, and found our way inside. It was the same as it always was. The remnants of cold cuts and what looked like a couple leftover slices of apple pie lingered in the air. I looked around. Three of the brick walls were bare, the fourth was adorned with posters and pamphlets for housing resources, counseling services, and food stamp applications. By this time the tables were only speckled with people. The majority had dispersed back into the shadows of the streets.

I didn't see Pastor Jim, but did notice a familiar face wearing a white clerical collar under a clean black blazer across the room, sitting in conversation. It was someone I had seen a few times when I used to come for meals. I walked over as Jeff watched and waited. I sat down a couple seats away, waiting for my chance for a conversation. He was talking with three young people who couldn't be much out of high school, two girls and a guy, probably close to the age I was when I was on the street. My eyes filled with water. My heart sank. I found myself in silent prayer, something I hadn't done in years. *Dear Lord, please guide them to safety.* I felt a lump gather in my throat. It was all too familiar.

I sat silently watching, wanting to reach out and help. I wanted to share with them all I had learned—the few tricks of the trade I had picked up in my short life sleeping on the hard ground—in my time scratching and clawing my way back onto my feet. I felt compelled to do more than observe.

I slowly stood up and walked over to the four of them. I squatted down at the end of the table quietly and waited to be invited into their discussion. One of the girls looked at me and smiled, but then turned back to the pastor. A minute later, the pastor turned to me, "Well, young man, how may I help you?" The other three group members got up and turned to leave.

"Wait," I said softly. They turned and looked my way. "Um—" I blinked and then introduced myself. They returned the favor. "Yeah, well, I'm not quite sure what to say, but I feel like I have to say something."

"Oh, what about?" The pastor asked.

"Well, I was homeless for a while... when I was about your guys' age," I said, looking at the three teens.

"We're not quite homeless," one of the girls replied. "One of our friend's moms set up beds in their garage."

"Sounds familiar. I had a spot on friends' couches for a little while too. And then I didn't."

"Where you living now?" the other girl asked.

"I live in an apartment near campus. I'm in college now."

"Wow—cool," the first girl said.

"I wanted to tell you that it's possible to change your life—to get on track again."

The three of them and the pastor sat and listened as I told my story. I started from the beginning—at least the beginning of this part of my life—from when my parents shut me out and I had to leave school. I told them about Christopher House and about a few other resources I came across as I was working my head back above water. I talked for, I don't know how long. They sat and listened intently. The pastor sat with a reassuring smile on his face, nodding occasionally. The young ones were quiet, but hung on every word. Every once in a while an *ooh* or an *ahh* would escape one of their mouths.

When I was done I made sure they had a place to go during the day, a place to wash up, a safe place to hang out or get help when needed. I gave them two different addresses, Christopher House and another separate support service that provided both men and women with some lodging possibilities.

As we got up to leave, the pastor asked me to stay a moment longer. He asked me if I would be willing to talk to a youth group at his church about my experiences. After I fumbled with my words for a moment I accepted and then, suddenly, remembered my original reason for wanting to talk to him. We spent a few minutes talking about my research and when we were done he handed me his card and I gave him my cell phone number. Underneath the name of his church was his name, Pastor Pete Smith, his phone number, and the address of the church.

"Thanks for the time, Pastor."

"Any time. I look forward to seeing you again."

He told me he would contact me in the next week to set up a time to meet with his youth group. I thanked him and we shook hands.

I met back up with Jeff and before I could apologize for talking so long, he asked me how it went. He seemed eager to know.

"It was amazing," I replied and I shared the details of my conversation as we headed out.

We decided to take a break and get something to eat. We found a small cafe I had passed dozens of times, but could never enter. Fortunately, once I tasted the food, it wasn't anything special, so I was able to convince myself that my never having been there before wasn't a big deal.

By the time we were done eating the line at the mission had started to form for the four-thirty dinner. "They line up early, don't they?" Jeff asked as he examined the line of people with interest.

"Yeah, people usually start showing up between three and three-thirty. They don't usually run out of food, but the pickins are better early on."

We walked by the growing line of nameless people. I peered at the faces as I passed, most of whom were unfamiliar, but I did see two I thought I recognized from my days standing in line. My heart skipped a beat. It seemed so long ago, and they were still there. They looked worn out and destitute as if they had accepted this life. I felt a trembling deep within, lowered my head, and tried to control my welling tears.

We walked for a while. I took him around my old hunting ground. I showed him the prime locations to find different food items—behind a bakery—a dumpster near a corner market—and my favorite, the garbage cans next to a steakhouse. I showed him the back alley where the big dope dealers hung out and then where I saw my first drug overdose. I explained how I found the person all alone, writhing on the ground in a pile of his own vomit.

"What'd you do?"

"There wasn't much I could do. I was helpless. It was almost dark, and I was tired and hungry. I couldn't call anyone. There weren't any cops or doctors around. In fact, at that moment, it felt like the streets were deserted. I looked around and saw one person walking into an open door across the street and a car drove by, but, for some reason, it was eerily quiet."

"Man, I can't imagine."

"Good. You don't want to."

We continued walking around the bustling streets, watching well-dressed business people scurrying here and there, in and out of tall buildings, moving with purpose. We went inside a souvenir shop, purchased a couple of cold drinks, and sipped them as we continued our venture around town. This was nothing new for either of us. I had been here often as a young boy with my family and Jeff, who was from out of town originally, had visited on a number of occasions too. There was always something interesting to see—the open market overlooking the waterfront, walking along the pier, partaking in whatever holiday celebration the time of year called for. But, we were looking at it with a different lens today. Obviously, I had spent intimate time here and had witnessed it from an angle a growing population of people were unfortunate enough to also be sharing. And, from the expression on Jeff's face, from the few comments he could muster, he was now seeing it from a new perspective, as well.

In and amongst, but not seen, the world hovered around, but did not include the masses in the shadows—in the cracks and creases of the city. After talking to Jeff a day later, he felt he had put on magic glasses that allowed him to see what was at first hidden. Like watching a nature show about animals with the ability to camouflage for survival, the unnamed, the faceless, the lost thousands lay hidden in plain sight. He described the horror he felt turning a corner and noticing suffering faces and knowing they had always been there and he had not noticed them before. And then he would turn another corner and they would appear again, faces, not the same, yet the same.

The day moved from late afternoon to early evening and then to evening. We were engrossed in our sightseeing journey, magic glasses and all, noticing, seeing, few words spoken, but those few words were more powerful than any words we had spoken to each other before—each sentence, each word, each syllable carried with it a life's worth of emotions.

We came to rest, sandwiched between a dozen other walkers at a crosswalk. Jeff took my hand and guided me through the people, out of the way, and to the side of a brick building. We stood facing each other. He looked out of breath, yet seemed not to be breathing. He seemed lost for words, yet seemed to be bursting with things to say.

"How—" He dropped his gaze and then looked back up, a determined look on his face. "How did you do it—how did you—" He searched for the right word. "How did you survive?" He looked pleadingly at me as if I held the answers to life's ever-evading riddles.

I shook my head slowly, took a deep breath, and pursed my lips. "Honestly, I don't know. I can explain a lot once I found the resources I needed. But, those first few weeks alone— alone in the cold—" I paused—shook my head more adamantly. "That's not totally accurate." He stood in front of me, intently waiting, listening. "I hid, like many of the homeless. I kept out of the way. I used my primal survival instincts and stayed away from anything that didn't look good. And then, after I gained a bit of courage, I watched. I listened. I took mental notes."

I rocked my head back and forth, but stood firm while I conjured images and emotions, while they rose within me, while my past overtook me. He took my hand and I continued my soliloquy. "A couple weeks in, I came out of my shell just enough to learn the things I needed to survive. I learned the best place to pitch my tent—how to keep my belongings from getting stolen—where and when to find food. And I learned who to talk to and who to stay away from." His hands quivered. "Finally, I learned that I wasn't going to let this be it—my life— the end—whatever. I was going to turn it around. Then, I was no longer just coming out of my shell. I had fully emerged and was taking my life back. That's when I connected with Pastor Jim at the mission and he led me to Christopher House."

"Holy, fuck. You—are—amazing." He pulled me close and embraced me. I felt tears welling again and my legs became weak. I had done this, for the most part, on my own, and it felt good to finally have someone by my side—to have someone comforting me—to have someone literally supporting me.

I let go of everything—years of pent-up anger, fear, and sorrow. My knees buckled—Jeff caught me and slowly lowered me to the ground, there, next to the brick facade of the building, next to a line of street homes—a few tents, dirty blue tarps, and a sleeping bag caked in dirt. We were both on our knees, my arms limp, his holding me tight. We blended in with the unseen homeless population on the sidewalk next to the brick wall people walked by every day. I began to sob uncontrollably— tears streaming down my face. The relief was like nothing I had experienced before.

I felt his hand rubbing my back as he held me. "It's okay… let it out," he whispered in my ear. "You're safe now."

My chest heaved in and out. My unsteady breaths echoed in my head. I struggled to find air. Erratic breaths wheezed in—and then out—and then in again. I worked to control my emotions. I took a shaky breath and drew it deep into my lungs. I repeated this several times and started to regain control of my body. I lifted my arms and hugged him back. We stayed there for a little while longer, holding each other, alone among the throngs of passersby—unseen among the makeshift abodes, and the dirty masses who called them home.

After some time, I slowly let go and Jeff loosened his hold. We stood back up and looked at each other, not quite sure what to say. I wiped my eyes and gave him a shy smile, my breathing somewhat under control. I looked at him and silently reached my hand toward his and motioned with my head to begin walking again. We walked for a couple of blocks, hand in hand, quietly taking in our surroundings with no destination in mind.

"Well, I guess I had a lot pent up," I said a few minutes later. Jeff looked at me and smiled. I took a deep breath. "Hmmm." I let out a satisfying groan. "It felt good." I stopped and pulled Jeff's hand. He stopped and looked at me. "I feel kind of strange, though... I'm not really sure how to react to what just happened. But, I do feel better." I could see Jeff wanted to say something, but he wasn't quite sure what. "Thanks." I finally said.

"You're welcome," he said sincerely, as we stood there, trying to figure out what to do next.

"I have one more stop I want to make." I turned and looked at him, still holding his hand. "You up for it?"

"Well, I'm sure another curveball won't hurt," he grinned.

"It's gonna be the toughest part of our day."

"Ooh—you did say you wanted to go back to the alley—I'll be okay." He pulled me towards him slightly. "Are you going to be okay?

"I think so," I replied, not knowing if that was true.

As we walked closer to my old home, a tingling sensation circulated my body and, in order to control my rising tension, I began talking nonstop, telling Jeff what to expect, telling him that by the time we made it to the alley many of its inhabitants will have made their way back for the night. It was a perfect time to see the hustle and bustle—to see the hidden figures living their lives off the beaten path, away from the businessmen and women departing from work—in what you might call the underworld of the city. While this was a good way to prepare Jeff for the experience, at least as much as it was possible to prepare him, it was really for my benefit, helping me process my emotions as we neared the encampment.

We still had quite a bit of sunlight left and would be able to witness life as it truly was. Fortunately, the heat of the rays had warmed the blacktop, which was radiating an invisible comfort—this was the time of year to be homeless, if there was such a thing.

I guided Jeff a few blocks north—across two intersections, through an adjacent alley— and then stopped abruptly and was home once again. *Are you ready?* I meant to say this out loud, but the voice only echoed inside my head. I think I was preparing myself for what was to come—warning myself that this was it, the pinnacle of our day, the emotional climax.

We looked at each other, silently nodded, and walked a few more feet until the buildings on our left opened up to a different world. We stood and peered in. It took a moment, but my body began to react to the reunion—heart pumping double time, sending blood at breakneck speed through my veins. Makeshift homes were crowded together from end to end on either side of the alley, leaving a walkway in between just wide enough for a single person to walk abreast. Off in the distance, we could see the other end. Yet, even though it was the same length as all the other alleys, it seemed twice as long. The corridor was so full that it appeared to encapsulate its own ecosystem, it was its own world within the larger world. It contained what seemed like its own dimension, something trapped within the world we lived in every day—a secret, hidden place where a new species of beings lived and survived, ignored by the world that hovered around it.

I turned to Jeff and quietly pointed out things I remembered, that once were home, but now seemed surreal—the doorway where the dope dealer camped out a couple times a week—the dumpster where people fought over scraps from the restaurant around the corner. I took a step in and led him by the hand, through piles of garbage, by dirty street people warming scraps on garbage can fires, by a couple who looked to be around sixteen sitting on the ground. The air was full with stale urine and rotten meat. Flies buzzed in masses. Three seagulls swarmed a half-eaten sandwich.

Two-thirds of the way through I stopped. Without making it obvious I pointed out the spot where a blue tarp was stretched from the edge of a garbage can to the top of a shopping cart. I told Jeff that this was the spot where I pitched my tent, most nights. I looked at him and smiled an uncomfortable smile, awkwardly trying to be both tour guide and level-headed recovering ex-street dweller. "Hard to believe," I said under my breath.

I let go of his hand and turned a slow three-sixty, taking in my surroundings as if I were from out of town. I felt emotional, but had nothing left to let out. My eyes stayed dry. My breathing was steady. I did hear a faint buzzing in my ear, but nothing more.

Jeff followed my lead as I slowly walked to the end of the alley and turned around to take one last look. We stood there, side by side, gazing down the crowded time capsule. We watched the sun vanish behind a tall building off in the distance, throwing a long shadow onto the ground, creating an ominous haze over the hidden world. I was emotionally spent and ready for the day to end, yet strangely ready for more.

I turned to Jeff. "Thanks for coming with me today."

"It was a great adventure," Jeff said as he reached over and put his hand on my shoulder. "Something I wasn't expecting."

"I wouldn't have been able to make it without you."

"I'm just glad I was able to be a part of it."

I reached over and put my arm around his waist. I've got

to find a way to get involved," I said as we turned and began walking down the sidewalk, heading in the direction of Jeff's car. "I've thought about it before and I just can't walk away without doing something."

"I'm sure we can find a way to make a difference," he added.

"Hmmm," I grunted curiously, "I'm sure we can," repeating the nominative pronoun, we, and letting it sink in.

* * *

We pulled up in front of my place about nine-thirty, more than twelve hours since we set off on our adventure. The sky was a faint gray and the crescent moon was high above my apartment building.

The car idled for a moment and then Jeff turned the key and it was silent. We both sat there, neither able to initiate conversation or end the day. I stared at my lap, my body feeling heavy. Finally, without really knowing what was coming out, I opened my mouth, "That was an adventure. I'm glad you were there."

There was a slight pause before Jeff fumbled with a few words, "It was—it was unexpected... but—but interesting—interestingly fulfilling." I turned and looked at him. He met my gaze. And then we both turned away. "I wouldn't have noticed all that without you," he continued. "I can't get those images out of my mind."

"Did you mean what you said when you said we?" I waited for a response. "Did you really mean that you want to do some volunteering with me?"

"I was caught up in the moment, I think. I didn't really know what I was saying." He shook his head slowly. "But, I think so.

I want to give it a shot anyway—I think it's important."

I began to think out loud, "I'm not exactly sure what I want to do, but I'm going to figure it out. I was thinking a good place to start would be to contact the church I attended the last few months I was on the street. I know they do some meal delivery and host a soup line once a month."

"Yeah. That seems like a good idea."

"I'll text you the info when I get it?"

"Or we can discuss it over lunch sometime."

I looked at him and smiled, "We can do that."

We sat there again, letting the silence overtake us. I slowly moved my left hand and set it on the emergency brake that sat between us, nervously inviting his touch. He placed his hand on mine.

Chapter Fifteen

I started seeing Jeff on a somewhat regular basis after that emotional trip to the alley downtown almost two weeks ago. We spent a couple days a week having morning coffee before classes and studying late at night in the library. Our time together had become more relaxed, although our conversations were still interspersed with periods of awkward silence. We knew we enjoyed spending time together, but still had not quite figured each other out.

On this day, we were following up on our plans to start volunteering. We were meeting Pastor Jim to help serve dinner at his church a mile from Christopher House. The church, an old brick building under a ceramic tiled roof, and a spire housing a weathered bell, sat at the far corner of the parking lot. We found a place to park and made our way inside. It always amazed me how all old churches smelled the same—years of dust and old Bibles. We walked into the foyer that sat in front of a large double door of windows looking into the sanctuary. A soft light flowed through the stained glass windows and fell upon the wooden pews lending a majestic air to the empty room as dust particles danced in the rays of light.

We found Pastor Jim and a few others in a back room near the kitchen and fellowship hall. They were sorting through food and paper goods.

"Hey, Pastor," I called across the room.

"Hey, you made it." He walked over and shook my hand. "You're sure looking good."

"Thanks."

"And this must be Jeff?"

"Yeah, Jeff, this is Pastor Jim." I motioned from Jeff to Pastor. They shook hands.

Pastor Jim turned around and introduced us to the other three volunteers.

"We're expecting a couple more helpers," he said. We should have more than enough volunteers this evening," He added.

We joined in the preparations—making sandwiches— organizing cutlery, plates, and napkins—setting up tables and chairs. It was an enjoyable time, but even so, the experience triggered a new set of memories and emotions, though I was much more prepared to handle them now. Fortunately, that visit, my first visit back to the lowest point in my young life, made it possible for me to deal with it and move on. While I wasn't totally beyond it, and may never be, I was in a better spot emotionally. In fact, my last two visits with my counselor made it apparent that tracing the steps of a life I had tried to forget was the right thing to do. I told him the whole ordeal, from my visits to Christopher House and the mission to my emotional breakdown and my walk through the alley. He reassured me that confronting my memories and emotions head-on is one of the best ways to heal. Helping others who were currently in the spot I used to be, was another. I had been going to counseling once a week for a month and a half and making great strides. There were still a few things I needed to deal with, and my counselor told me that, over time, those things would surface and he would help me deal with them too.

It was a few minutes before five and a line of people had gathered outside the church and was growing rapidly. Jeff and I looked out the window and guessed that at least thirty people were waiting patiently. A few minutes later we took another look and the number had more than doubled. By the time the doors opened, there were close to eighty people.

Jeff and I worked the food table, handing out sandwiches, apples, celery sticks, and carrots. Pastor told us that it was not just food these people needed. They also needed human interaction. They needed to be treated with dignity and to feel like they matter. So, we worked quickly, but made sure to look each person in the eyes and say a few nice words to them as they shuffled by and filled their plates.

People of all ages gathered for the meal—people over sixty, people in their twenties and thirties, and everything in between. There were a few moms with children and a couple complete families, including a mom and dad with four children. It was both heartwarming to do the work, but heartbreaking to see so many people in need. The hardest part was knowing that this was just a fraction of the people teaming the streets or living in shelters. With each plate served, my resolve grew stronger and I knew this was not all that needed to be done. I told myself that I would find more. I would do more. I would not walk away and let this be it.

After all the food was served, a few people sat around finishing up. Jeff and I made our way around and asked each person how they were doing. We sat next to the couple with four children. They were amazingly upbeat. They told us that they lived in a low-rent apartment about a mile away and that they made it to as many of these types of meals as possible.

Both of them had jobs and received a little bit of government assistance, but most of their money was taken up with rent and bills. They told us that the food they received at the mission and the church was both a blessing and a lifesaver. My eyes filled with tears as I watched their kids smile with each bite and then run around the room giggling and laughing when they were done eating. I walked over to their youngest and handed her the last apple on the table. She reached her hand out gently and then ran over to one of her brothers holding the apple high above her head, showing it to him with joy. They continued running around, playing a makeshift game of tag, while the youngest protected her little red prize.

As the room emptied, we began cleaning up. I walked around sweeping crumbs off the floor while Jeff wiped down the tables and chairs. My head was buzzing with emotions, yet this time the emotions were external to myself. I was finally able to separate myself from the homelessness, something I felt I had to do in order to do my part. I felt driven by my experiences, but those experiences no longer defined who I was. I felt I had more control over my life and was able to make a difference.

The following week I became obsessed with my research paper and spent almost every night for two weeks either in a cubicle with my laptop, sitting next to Jeff, or on the small table in my apartment reading, taking notes, and transcribing my interviews. I became addicted to coffee and pretzels in order to push through and when I finally turned in my paper, I felt like I went through caffeine withdrawals.

One evening Jeff and I were walking to the library when a voice caught our attention. We turned to see Tim jogging our way, Joey following behind.

"Hey, Tim. What's up?" I said with excitement.

"That should be my question, " Tim replied, catching his breath.

Jeff and I looked at each other and smiled. "Whaddya mean?" Jeff said sarcastically, as we were both aware that it was probably a bit strange seeing us enjoying each other's company. The last time Tim and Joey saw us, Jeff didn't want anything to do with me. In fact, recently, we talked about how we would have some explaining to do the next time we saw them.

"Nice to see you guys getting along," Tim said.

"If I'm not mistaken," Joey butted in, "this doesn't look to be a chance meeting between you two."

"You might say that," Jeff said as he shot me a quick wink.

"What're we missing here?" Tim inquired with curiosity.

"Missing? What would you be missing?" I chimed in playfully.

"Yeah, right—okay. Nothing to see here, I'm sure," Tim scoffed, looking at Joey for support.

"Yeah—yeah—right—nothing going on," Joey laughed as he reached out and gently pushed Jeff's shoulder.

"We've just been studying together a bit," I said in defense.

"Studying—that's right—we've been studying," Jeff laughed.

We continued our playful banter a few more minutes and then ended up heading to the pub across the quad—the first break from my paper I had in over a week. It felt good to forget about schoolwork for a while and it was nice to catch up with Tim and Joey.

We entered the pub and a soft voice coming from the far end of the bar floated out of a set of speakers on either side of a small stage and enveloped us as we walked to a booth in the middle of the room. It was open mic night—an amateur singer, slam poetry, and a guitar player accompanied by a drum and a young man singing the cover of a song I didn't recognize. It was the guitar player who stood out to me. He was good, but it was his face—a face I was sure I had seen sitting in the front section of my psych class. It's interesting to see a different side of someone who you had crossed paths with on occasion. You never know what's hidden beneath.

I looked over at Jeff. He was sharing the story of our meeting at the coffee house that led to the Saturday bike trip, then our day retracing my life through the downtown streets. The other two listened intently, posing thoughtful questions now and then.

"So, what's your guys' situation?" Joey finally asked.

"What do you mean, situation?" I said, returning the question with a flippant grin. "We're not in a situation," I laughed. "We're just a couple guys hanging out."

We all laughed. Joey and Tim shot me a sarcastic glance. Jeff placed his hand on my knee. "Just hanging out, like he said."

I put my hand on his. "Like I said, just hanging out," I winked.

"Okay, if you don't want to go into details, we get it. Don't we Joey?"

"Of course we do." Joey paused, stood up, leaned in, and whispered loudly, "But that ain't going to keep us from prying." He laughed. We all joined in the frivolity.

I looked at my watch, "Doesn't look like we're getting much studying done tonight. Want to order drinks?" It didn't take much to talk them into it and soon we each had a sudsy lager in hand.

We sat for a while, catching each other up on the last couple months, sipping beers, and laughing. It was the first time in my life I felt myself—the first time I felt I could be who I wanted to be—and so I did a U-turn and headed back to the topic that started our conversation. "So, to be honest—" They turned and looked at me. "We've been hanging out a lot." All three nodded their heads. "In fact, I wouldn't be in the place I am today without him."

"Oh, okay," Tim said with a slight nod, eyebrows raised.

"Yeah, nice to hear," Joey added. "We thought we missed the mark when it didn't work out the first time you guys met."

"You had us marked, huh?" I peered at them out of the corner of my eye. "I guess it just took time. Things have a way of working themselves out—and it was sure good to have him with me when I went downtown. That, and a couple months of counseling got me feeling like I'm on the right path for the first time."

Jeff leaned over and put his arm around my shoulders and turned his head toward me. "Glad I was with you, too." He turned to Tim and Joey, "It was a life-changing experience for both of us."

We sat quietly, sentimentality setting in.

"Well," Tim said with conviction. "It's nice to know you guys are happy." He nodded and smiled. "But," he added with flair, "enough of this emotional stuff. Time for another round." He laughed as he stood up and looked at us in turn, "I'll get the next one, but you guys owe me." He patted his chest with his open palm and walked over to the bar with a strut.

We stayed at the pub for a few hours—talking, drinking, laughing, and finally dancing—Jeff and I playfully dancing with each other for the first time. Tim and Joey dancing with two undergrads who they met at the bar.

That was the only break I had from studying for two weeks—that and a conversation with my sister about Jeff and my trip downtown. I had another good cry as I heard her tears flowing over the phone.

"I'm going to visit you soon," she said as our conversation was coming to an end.

"I'd like that," I said with a quivering voice. "I'll introduce you to Jeff."

* * *

Two days later, I finished my paper. Before I turned it in, Jeff read it over for me while I watched him intently, looking for any visual sign that what I had written was nothing short of a masterpiece.

We were sitting on the edge of my bed in my apartment. When he finished reading, he set the paper down on the side table, rested his elbows on his knees, and put his face in his hands. He breathed in and exhaled. "I'm not sure if it's because I watched you walk the streets—because I saw you physically in that environment—but I could see you clearly on each page, in each word—and I could see the faces—the faces from the streets." He paused to catch his breath. "It read like a Greek tragedy, like poetry, like a horror story." He shook his head.

I walked over to the kitchen, grabbed one of the three cups on the shelf, and filled it with water from a pitcher in the fridge. The filling cup gurgled. I walked back over to Jeff and handed him the cup.

"Thanks," he said. And we sat in silence.

* * *

At the end of the semester, my sister came to visit. She drove up in Mom's old silver Ford Focus. It still had the ding on the passenger side bumper from when my dad was trying to teach me to parallel park and I hit the light pole outside our house.

It was almost dinner time, so we ordered pizza and stayed up watching movies and getting reacquainted. We had only seen each other a couple times over the past few years and it seemed like a lifetime ago we lived in the same house, sharing the bathroom between our rooms, fighting over the remote and the comfy chair next to the fireplace.

She asked me if Jeff was my first boyfriend. I told her about Kelly, about how he went with me to visit Dad in the hospital, and how he was a great friend, but after a night out and a passionate kiss, we knew we were just that. Jeff, on the other hand, I told her, was a bit of an enigma.

"What do you mean?" she asked.

"Well, when I first met him, he wasn't very nice. Whenever I came around he would leave in a huff."

"Oh, a sure sign of love." She winked.

"The first night I met him he saw me with Kelly. Later, I found out he was just jealous." I shrugged. "But I'm still not quite sure. We spend a lot of time together. And, we've shared a lot."

"From what you've told me, it seems like the relationship is worth pursuing."

"Yeah, it is—but enough about me. What are you up to?"

"Finally figuring a few things out. Got a reception job at the Doctor's office by our house. Been there for about nine months and I'm planning on taking a few classes at the college. They have a medical assistant program that I'm interested in."

We talked all night, letting the TV play in the background, letting the few leftover slices of pizza get cold, and allowing ourselves to slip back into memories from the past while not letting go of our current selves. We were sitting on the couch, facing each other, warmth radiating between us.

"You remember when we stayed up playing video games and then snuck downstairs and ate all the leftover Halloween candy?" my sister asked.

"Yeah, you were in fifth grade, I think."

Looking down at her lap, she continued—"You stayed up all night holding my hair back as I puked it all up in the bathroom."

"Yup—and we still had to get up for Sunday school the next morning." We both chuckled.

She paused and then looked up, "Even though I thought I was going to puke up a lung, I remember how safe I felt with you there." She cocked her head and peered through sad eyes. "I've missed that." I looked at her and smiled and then nodded my head. Her voice quivered. "The house has felt cold ever since you left. You were the one who always made me feel good, like nothing bad was ever going to happen, even when Dad went into one of his tirades." She closed her eyes and took a small, quick breath in, opened her eyes, and let it out. "Dad fell apart and was mad all the time once you were gone."

"Well, he wasn't far from gone when I was there," I winked.

"True," she said in agreement, nodding her head and pausing for a moment to ingest this reality. "Whenever things got out of hand, you had a way of calming things down, though." She stopped to stifle a tear. "You would bring me into your room and turn on the music or play a game with me. You would take Mom into a different room and shield her from Dad's anger, like that time you asked her to help us make Christmas cookies and we spent the rest of the night literally covered in flower and vanilla extract while dad stewed in anger watching a football game." We sat as the TV droned on. Memories floated between us. "I sure wish Mom could just relax, especially now that Dad's gone." She looked up at the ceiling in deep thought. "She was so dependent on him and got so used to the tension in the house. I'm sure she doesn't know anything else. But, I'm also sure she knows how bad things were, but didn't know what to do—and still doesn't."

"Well," I said softly, looking off into the distance. "I decided a while ago that I was going to live my life." I turned toward her and spoke with more conviction. "The way I got off the street was deciding to take my life into my own hands. Once I figured a few things out, I made sure I did everything in my power to move my life forward." The TV went silent as a movie ended and the credits rolled up the screen. "I love you, sis. I want to be there for you, but—but I got to live my life. I can't go back and try to save something that I have worked so hard to put behind me."

A lone tear slowly made its way down her left cheek. "I know—I get it." Her voice trembled.

"You need to forget about Mom for a while and think about yourself. You deserve a good life. If she can't get it together, you can't let her pull you down with her."

She closed her eyes. Tears streamed down her face.

"Hey," I reached out and put my hand on her leg. "Just because I'm not going back to that old life—just because I'm not going to try to save Mom—doesn't mean you and I can't still be a family." She opened her eyes and looked at me. "I'm still your big brother."

She let out a sigh and a breathy giggle. I leaned over and put my arms around her. We hugged for a long time.

* * *

I woke the next morning, huddled with a few blankets on the floor, my sister sitting on the edge of the pull-out bed, and the smell of coffee filling the room. She got up and poured me a cup and we sat for a while enjoying each other's company. We spent the day together. I walked her around campus and we got a bite to eat at the pub.

"You ever going to introduce me to Jeff?" She asked, as we finished our lunch.

"He's visiting some friends out of town, but should be back this evening. I can see if he's free."

"That'd be nice. I'd like to meet the guy who's spending so much time with my big brother."

I pulled out my phone and sent a quick text. A few minutes later, my pocket vibrated and we had a dinner date set for six.

I finished showing her around campus, where most of my classes were held, and the atrium that was in the center of campus. We walked to the north side of campus and looked down into the valley that was filled with trees and a large river off in the distance. The sun was high in the sky and warmed our backs as we stood admiring the view.

"Can you take me downtown sometime and show me where you used to sleep?" My sister said gently, with kind curiosity. "I don't want to make you uncomfortable, but I feel like I need to see it."

"Yeah, sometime." I turned and looked at her, hiding the nervous bubbles floating in my stomach, still struggling with the idea of sharing that tragic time in my life.

We spent the next hour sitting on the steps that led from the quad to an expansive water feature and a large marble sculpture of a man running with his hands in the air. The sun covered us with warmth as we talked about little to nothing, but shared in the comfort of the moment, while I tried to get passed my conflicted emotions—emotions I later came to realize would always be a part of who I am.

* * *

At six we arrived at Jeff's apartment in Mom's beat-up Ford. I pulled out my phone and texted Jeff and stood outside the car waiting. He finally emerged from the building. I walked over and we gave each other a quick hug. As we turned toward the car my sister was standing by her door with an eager smile on her face.

"Sis, this is Jeff," I said in a somewhat truncated introduction.

Jeff reached out and shook her hand. "Nice to meet you," he nodded.

"I've heard a lot about you." She smiled at him and then turned to me with a reassuring grin. "—well, actually, more about how much time you guys have been spending together."

"That's true. We've seen a lot of each other the last few weeks," he said.

We stood there, looking at each other.

"What are you guys up for eating tonight?" I finally asked.

"Doesn't matter to me," my sister replied. "I'm just looking forward to spending more time with my big brother and getting to know the guy who's been taking up so much of his time," she said playfully.

"There's a great little Italian restaurant just down the road," Jeff suggested. "There may be a bit of a line, but it's worth the wait." He navigated from the back seat, telling my sister which way to turn, leaning forward between the seats, reaching his hand out, and pointing to the parking lot across the street as we got closer to the restaurant. "Get your taste buds ready," he boasted. "You're in for a treat."

We walked across the street to a small strip mall that housed the restaurant, a souvenir shop, a few different clothing stores, and a bank. Jeff led the way to the front door, pulled it open, and invited us in. We were hit with the aroma of warm bread and garlic and my stomach roared to life, demanding to be fed.

The restaurant was full. We sat shoulder to shoulder for thirty minutes on a small bench in front of a chalkboard sign that read, *please wait to be seated*. Finally, we were escorted to a table at the far end of the small dining room. We shared conversation over soft bread and butter as we looked over the menu. We talked about the difficulty of choosing a baked dish over a regular dish, seafood over chicken, noodles over dumplings—and we curbed our appetite with the soft white warmth that melted the butter as they came in contact.

"So, you're from out of town originally, my brother tells me." Once the matter of food was out of the way my sister quickly turned the interrogation light toward Jeff.

"Yeah, about an hour south of here."

"What made you want to go to school in the city?" she continued.

"I've always liked it here. My parents brought me and my brother here quite a bit. We would walk the pier, go to a show once in a while, and even saw The Nutcracker at the opera house when I was in middle school."

"The Nutcracker?" I chimed in. "We've never been to the opera house."

"It was an eye-opener. Probably the thing that attracted me here," Jeff said. "Lots of lights. Everyone dressed up. It was the first big event we did in the city."

"Sounds fun," my sister added. "Wish our parents took us to stuff like that. We did go to a couple museums, but nothing glamorous."

"It was also the first time I wore a tie. I felt grown up and we got to eat little snacks and drink tea. Good memories."

"So, what are you studying?" She continued grilling him.

"Economics—took me a while to narrow it down. I like data. I like projections. I like numbers. Was thinking about majoring in math, but I'm looking into being a financial planner or maybe an accountant."

"That sounds interesting," she responded.

"What's with all the questions, sis?"

"Just trying to make sure you're spending time with the right people. Someone's gotta do it and it sure ain't gonna be Mom," She raised her eyebrows and shrugged, only half joking.

"It's okay. Glad to help out," Jeff chuckled.

Our food was served and the conversation stopped as we filled our mouths with bitefuls of buttery cheese and pasta. I looked up from my plate, first at my sister, who returned a grin through a mouthful of chicken penne, and then at Jeff who had a smudge of sauce on his cheek. I gave him a nod and gestured with my napkin. He leaned toward me with a little smirk. I reached out and softly dabbed his face. Our eyes met and the sudden intimacy of the moment surprised me—my heart sped up and I could feel my blood racing through my body.

We continued eating, talking a little in between bites—about this, about that, about nothing in particular—but it was relaxing—it was enjoyable—it was not forced and there was no agenda. We shared the meal and the time together, relaxing over drinks after our plates were cleared from the table, ending the night only when the lights had been dimmed and we realized we were the last ones in the restaurant.

* * *

It became a regular thing—our time together. I would be at Jeff's place. He would be at mine. Or we would be somewhere on campus, talking, holding hands, sipping tea or coffee. When fall came and classes began, our routine shifted. I was receiving credit for an internship twice a week at an organization supporting homeless teens and Jeff had a part-time job at an accounting firm, running errands and getting coffee for the opposite crowd, men and women in suits and ties going to meetings in tall buildings downtown. We organized our time together between classes and work, meeting most of the time at the library or pub on campus, but once in a while, Jeff would join me, volunteering his time with the homeless teens. He said he enjoyed that more than serving coffee to the rich, but the money he earned stirring cream and sugar into the addicting black liquid made it bearable.

By the time Christmas rolled around, we were both just a few credits shy of graduation and we started talking about what we wanted to do after we were done. We knew that neither of us wanted to go home for the holidays, something he had done each winter, something I had never done. We were sitting in my small studio apartment, shoes off, feet up on the coffee table, my head leaning on his shoulder, watching light flakes of snow dance in the wind outside the one and only window on the cream-colored wall that displayed the many signs of former tenants.

"I think the first thing we should do is save a bit of money," Jeff said. "We've only got a few months left, but if we pool our resources we could have a small nest egg built up."

"Just to let you know Mr. Financial Advisor, I don't have much in the way of resources," I chided.

"You'd be surprised what you can do with what little you have."

"Okay, what are you thinking?"

"Well, it doesn't make sense that we're both paying rent when we spend so much time together."

"Hmmm... I see." I sat up and looked at him sarcastically. "You trying to coax me into a commitment," I shot him a crooked smile.

"Not necessarily." He responded with a light giggle. But you gotta agree" He put his hand on my shoulder. "We could save quite a bit if we only paid for one place."

"True," I nodded. "You been thinking about this for a while?"

"For a little while, anyway."

"I'm assuming, since you have the bigger place, I would join you."

"You could. Or I could join you here." He looked around.

"We couldn't fit much of your stuff in here, despite how lavish it is." We enjoyed a laugh.

"I thought we could consolidate—get rid of whatever we don't need or at least whatever we can do without."

"We would save more money if you moved in here." We sat for a moment. "And I can't say I haven't thought about it, " I confessed. We sat a little longer. I could see the gears in his head were churning double time. He was staring at the ceiling, nose furrowed, eyes squinted. "Whatcha thinking about?" I broke his concentration.

"How much stuff I can fit in my car on the way to Goodwill."

I got up and walked over to the other side of the room. "Wonder if we'd both be comfortable on this old pull-out bed."

"I guess we can pull it out and see," Jeff suggested.

Moments later we were side by side on what was just a love seat more than an actual couch, and now, a single bed more than a bed built for two. We scooched close together, and then I sat up, leaned to my left, and pulled a blanket from a drawer at the bottom of the side table. I laid back down and spread the blanket over the two of us. We cuddled together, but said nothing.

A minute later I raised my right arm and brought it over and behind Jeff's head. He turned on his side and moved closer to me. We laid motionless, quiet. The warmth of our bodies raising the temperature in the room.

"I think we can make this work," I said.

"Yeah. We can make this work," Jeff agreed.

* * *

The next three and a half months went by quickly, but were by far the best three months of my life. We emptied my apartment of every extra object—trinket, plate, cup, napkin, shoe—and stuffed it full of as much of Jeff's belongings as possible. We managed to squeeze everything he needed into the living area of the maybe three-hundred-square-foot apartment.

We spent every free minute together. I would drive him to work in his car and then drive back to school for my morning class on the days he was scheduled to serve coffee to the rich accountants on the twelfth floor of the sparkling building overlooking the bay downtown. He would accompany me working with the homeless teens on the days he didn't have class or work. The rest of the time we sat with each other on the loveseat, bed, or at the small table between the loveseat and kitchen, holding hands, kissing, watching late-night television, kissing, scrolling through our dream jobs on the internet, kissing, maybe doing homework, but if nothing else, kissing— and sometimes we would do a bit of homework.

After a few weeks, I felt like we could do this forever. We could find a small apartment in the city. We could find jobs doing what we wanted to do—me helping those on the streets—he helping those who had homes, who had money, who had everything else they needed. All we needed was each other and that's what I knew and that's how I felt and that's what I wanted.

One day as we scrolled through our dream jobs between kissing sessions, it popped up, something I never thought about before—an overseas position working in a third-world country, teaching elementary and middle school kids in a small village. It was temporary, but it was across the ocean, away from Jeff. I'm not sure why, I just read the posting, but I felt like it was calling me. It felt like something I needed to do. I sat, stewing in my own emotions, my heart pounding. A lump formed in my throat and I suddenly felt pulled in each direction, the desire to stay as close to Jeff as possible and the need to give this new opportunity a try. I needed to go, yet I wanted to stay. Finally, through the echo of fingers on his keyboard, I broke the silence.

"Jeff?" I said quietly. I paused for a moment. "I love you."

"Oh." He turned and looked at me, eyebrows raised. " I love you, too."

We had never said that to each other before. And I wasn't sure why I said it, except for maybe to soften the blow of what came next. "I found a job I want to apply for. It starts a few weeks after the semester ends."

"What is it?"

"Working with disadvantaged kids."

"That's right up your alley. Where is it at?"

"Ghana," I said sheepishly.

"Ooh—you mean the Ghana that's located in Africa?"

* * *

Later that week I met with my counselor. I told him I had applied to do some missionary work. He was happy for me. He told me I'd made great strides and a few months in a new environment may just be what the doctor ordered. In fact, he joked, "Those ARE the doctor's orders."

It felt good to be looking ahead, to be moving in a new direction, to have something to look forward to outside of my current world. But, I was nervous. If my application was accepted, I was concerned that it may be too much. Was I ready to take on the challenge? What would happen to Jeff and me? Questions circled through my mind. I shared them with my counselor. He said it was natural to be nervous and it was healthy to have questions. "The most important thing," he said, "is to trust your decisions. Questions are natural, but trust in self is key."

* * *

Two months later, Jeff and I were lying on the bed cuddled together—a Band-Aid on each of my shoulders covering the last of the shots I had to get in order to inoculate myself from unknown diseases and prepare my body for travel across the Atlantic to a country I knew little about—my newly purchased passport sitting on the small table by the kitchen, bags packed, crowded in between the front door and bathroom.

"How long until we have to leave?" Jeff asked.

"Fifteen minutes. I have to meet the rest of the group by TSA."

"How many are actually going?"

"Five, I think. And a group leader."

He turned toward me and wrapped me up with both arms. We laid there until it was just about time to go.

"Make sure you send me a couple pictures from graduation," I told him.

"For sure. I'll get one with Tim and Joey."

"And, stay in touch."

"I should be telling you the same thing. You're the one going to the other side of the world to take part in a once-in-a-lifetime opportunity. You're going to be so busy you might forget about me"

"You ain't going to get rid of me that easy." I sat up on the edge of the bed, my stomach filled with reservation—turning with anxiousness. I reached over and took his hand.

* * *

After a long hug among the throngs of travelers, we finally let go of each other, tears filling our eyes. I turned toward the TSA sign and noticed a few people gathering which I assumed were the people I would be spending the next three months with. I turned back to Jeff and gave him one last hug and kiss. I grabbed his hand, not wanting to let go. We stood, looking silently into each other's tear-stained faces. "I'm not sure how my cell service will be, but I'll send you texts and pictures whenever I can," I said as a consolation.

"I know you will." He struggled to smile. "Have a great time."

I squeezed his hand and then walked over and met with my group, introducing myself to each of them. I turned to capture one final image of Jeff—but he was gone.

Chapter Sixteen

It was an almost seventeen-hour flight with a four-hour layover in Portugal. I sat in a window seat next to a twenty-six-year-old grad student named Henry. He was taking a break from his international studies coursework "to experience the world," as he put it. We had a great time getting to know each other for the first hour, but then we checked our flight progress and realized we had a lot of time to fill, so we decided to take a nap.

When I woke, I looked over and Henry was reading a book with his earbuds tamped tight in his ears. I looked at my watch. I managed to take off just about two hours from our travel time. I pulled up the window shade and looked down to see a mass of clouds, and nothing else. I assumed we were somewhere over the Atlantic, but decided to let the plane do its thing and allow time to pass as best I could, so I turned on the TV in the headrest in front of me and flipped through the entertainment offerings. I found a few movies of interest, but instead, I decided to pick up my book and try to read for a while—although, whenever my voice echoed in my head all I could think about was Jeff. I closed my book and turned on a mindless comedy hoping to, if not cure, at least delay my sadness—and fortunately, it worked. After two movies, a hundred pages, and a meal, we were nearing our layover.

Four hours later we boarded a new plane on our final flight to Accra, the capital of Ghana. This time I sat next to a thirty-something named Cynthia. She told me she had been through a recent divorce and was using this experience to move on. By the time we landed and were sitting in a cramped bus on a bumpy road to a small village outside the capital city, I realized that our band of missionaries was an assortment of people from all walks of life. In addition to Henry and Cynthia, we had a Navy vet of twenty-nine named Jordan and a twenty-year-old who just had to put her final year of undergrad on hold when she heard about this opportunity.

About an hour later, the sky was dim and a few lights became visible up ahead. "We're almost there," our group leader said excitedly. We all started moving in our seats, craning our heads this way and that to catch a glimpse of our new temporary home.

We were warned that the living and educational systems we would be residing and working in during our time in Ghana were extremely subpar. We were even sent a few pictures and videos in our training packages, but nothing, other than witnessing it firsthand, would give us a true sense of the devastatingly difficult lives these poor families had to endure. We would be living in a small house with four bedrooms and a bathroom. A second building behind the house, separated by a small courtyard, had a kitchen and sitting room. We had all the basic necessities, but quickly realized that however basic our accommodations were, they were luxurious compared to the homes of the families and young students we would be working with.

During our third week in the village, I started to feel like I was getting the hang of things. I was teaching classes in the mornings, five days a week, two sessions of middle-level English and a session of middle-level history and geography. And, since I had played sports growing up, I taught sports classes in the afternoon, mainly fútbol. Luckily, I played soccer for a few years in elementary and middle school and knew what I was doing, for the most part.

One Wednesday afternoon, I was carrying our only three soccer balls out to the rocky dirt field behind the school we used for practices when I felt a sharp pain in my abdomen. I stopped briefly and looked down at my midsection—the pain subsided. I shook my head and then went about my business.

After dinner that night, I felt abnormally full and my body was fatigued. I chalked it up to the stress of getting settled in the new climate and then the sleepless nights, as I was having a difficult time sleeping more than two hours at a clip. Most nights, I would lie supine on my bed counting the metaphorical sheep until the next time my eyes were heavy enough to stay closed for another hundred and twenty minutes. I got into the habit of reading one of the four books I had with me when the sheep didn't work and would usually wake up with the book lying flat on my chest after I had read just a few pages.

I climbed in bed early and figured I'd sleep or at least rest the fatigue away. That night though, I fell asleep quickly and slept all the way until morning, waking up drenched in sweat and feeling no more rested than I did seven hours before. I forced myself to get up, took off my wet shirt, and pulled on a hooded sweatshirt. I went to the bathroom and sat on the toilet. I must have blacked out because the next thing I knew I woke with the back of my head resting on the wall behind me and the toilet full of brown liquid. I sat there trying to balance myself on the toilet seat as my head spun in circles. I took a few deep breaths, hoping to regain my senses—but, the next thing I remembered was waking up in bed with our group leader sitting in the chair next to me.

I spent the next week in a small hospital in an open room with three other patients. When I first arrived they told me I was exhibiting the symptoms of Malaria. It took four days to receive the test results, during which I took precautionary medication and lost twelve pounds from sitting on the toilet and sweating through my sheets twice a day. Eventually, the diagnosis was confirmed and, toward the end of the week, my symptoms started to dissipate. It did take a full two weeks to recover, the second of which was spent in my small room back in the village. But, I still wasn't strong enough to spend a full day teaching. And, soon after those two weeks, it was clear it would take a bit longer to regain enough strength to do any substantial work. By the time I was able to teach a half day, we had been there for almost two months. My fellow missionaries, our group leaders, and our hosts in the village wouldn't stop raving about how I handled my illness and how hard I worked to get back on my feet.

I chalked it up to my time on the streets and I told my story to them all one night at a faculty dinner. We were gathered at what they called, "apontow ma yɛn adamfofa" or "feast for our friendship. This was an annual celebration of the connection that was created during the three months the missionaries and villagers worked together. It was another transformative moment. Here I was, living with people I had just recently met, doing salt of the earth work with them hand in hand, in a country, in a village, in a culture foreign to anything I had ever been a part of, on the other side of the world, sharing my most intimate life stories.

The night went on until close to midnight with many others sharing. We laughed, cried, shook hands, hugged. We listened. We communed.

After many stories—after sharing in the experiences of my colleagues, both from America and Ghana, I felt privileged to be a part of this group of people. It made me see my life, my experiences, the difficulties I went through—the forced separation from my family, my time on the street—as a necessary part of my development.

Soon, I was back on my feet full-time and able to work all day for the final three weeks of our stay. I felt it a blessing to have endured my illness, just like it now felt like a blessing to have endured my time living in a makeshift home on the streets of a busy city.

Working with the young children who came from nothing, but also displayed nothing but gratitude—was nothing short of miraculous. The eagerness by which they engaged in daily lessons—coming to school shoeless, yet hearts full of desire, brimming with love and compassion—was inspirational—a blessing to witness and be a part of.

When the final day in our temporary village home seemed all too close, my heart began to ache. It was not dissimilar to the feeling I had leaving Jeff, but it was at such an intensity I was almost flattened for two nights. It was as if I was preparing to lose a loved one forever—as if I was getting ready to bury my own child. I spent the last two nights in bed, mourning the loss of my children and the friends I would be leaving behind. It was a profoundly sad feeling, but ultimately one I was glad I was able to experience. I did not fight it. I embraced it, along with everything else in my life. This trip to this small village taught me to see my feelings, my experiences, both good and bad, as part of who I am and who I will become. I allowed myself to cry deep and hard those final two nights, in bed by myself, which, in turn, allowed me to leave with sadness in my heart, but, more importantly, with peace of mind.

We drove away after breakfast on that last day, all huddled in the same small van we arrived in, on the same bumpy road, with the same driver escorting us back to the capital city, and back to the same airport where we would begin our journey home.

The entire village was standing outside the back window of the van, yelling goodbye, waving signs of thanks as we drove away, the five of us and our group leader holding hands, not a dry eye among us.

I took my phone out of my pocket and scrolled through the last few pictures. I clicked on a group shot—me with my students, my new Ghanaian friends and colleagues, and the other five friends who I met at the airport somewhere in Western Civilization and traveled with to the East to take part in something we never knew would be so life-changing. I smiled to myself and sent it to Jeff, with the caption, *beginning our journey home.* *Ping*—I looked at my phone. *Can't wait to see you,* he replied.

The next twenty-one hours were nothing like the original journey to a far-off land that felt like an expedition of discovery. Both flights home were relatively quiet. The eagerness to get to know each other, to talk about the adventure that was to come as we headed east, gave way to melancholy, to deep thought and reminiscing. Henry, who I spent the most time within the village, and I, used the time on our final flight to decompress, getting ourselves ready to reemerge into a life that now felt foreign and far away. We were high up above the floor of the world, suspended between realities—the one that once was—and the one that now is. At that moment though, we couldn't tell which was which as we were no longer the same people who we were just three months ago.

Finally, the captain came over the loudspeaker, "We are approaching our final destination, please prepare yourself for landing." He announced the weather and a sports score of a game that was currently being played a few hundred feet below. "A key game in the battle for the division title," he said, as the click–click of seat belts echoed in the fuselage.

Our seats shook softly as the plane began its slow descent back into our old life. It was as if we were warping back through time, back to a life once lived. A few minutes later, a low rumble below our feet as the landing gear came to life. I looked down at the armrest between Henry and me and put my hand on his. He looked over at me and smiled. "Hard to believe we're almost home," he said. I nodded my head as butterflies began to dance in my stomach.

We landed and taxied to our gate. I got up and stood in the line of people waiting to depart the plane and grabbed my luggage from the overhead compartment. I faced forward, staring at the back of the head of the person in front of me, and slowly followed as the line moved forward. A nod and a smile at the flight attendant who brought me meals and snacks over the past seven hours led me onto the loading bridge that connected the plane to the gate. As I walked, a soft wind blew through the jetway and an eerie feeling of time travel overtook me. It was as if I was being drawn back in time closer to my old life, yet my old self who existed in that life no longer existed. It felt odd. I felt like a player in a movie, in the story of a life that wasn't mine. I was ready to hit warp speed, for everything to blur, and to be transported to another time—another dimension.

I walked through the double doors and into the airport. I met with the other members of my group. We stood for a moment, looking at each other. We gathered in a small circle and held hands. We said our goodbyes with tears, but with fewer tears than we did when leaving the village. We all promised to keep in touch and then wound our way through the corridors of the airport to baggage claim and to our families and friends.

As I waited for my bags to come down the shoot, I stood on my tiptoes and swiveled my head around, looking for the familiar face that was scheduled to pick me up. I finally spotted his silhouette and called his name. He turned, smiled, and walked toward me with urgency. We came together and threw our arms around each other without saying a word. I closed my eyes and held him tight. It still felt like a dream. I was hoping when I opened my eyes everything would feel normal again. However, I opened them, blinked twice, and it was still a haze. I couldn't believe Jeff was standing in front of me—that I wasn't lying in my bed back in the village deep in a sleepless dream.

We stepped back from each other, still holding hands. "Let me look at you," he said.

"Not much to look at," I replied.

"Well, not as much as there was before you left," he said with a big smile on his face. "You're quite a bit leaner than you were—and I like the scruff on your face."

"I think you'll find that's not all that's changed."

"I can't wait to find out. I'm sure you have a lot of stories to tell."

"Once I get my bearings. My head is spinning. It's been a busy forty-eight hours."

"I'm sure. But, I do have a surprise to add to the excitement."

He stepped back and pointed passed a group of people behind him and there, with a big smile on her face, was my sister. She ran toward me, jumped in my arms, and squeezed me tight.

"Hey, brother. You look like you've been working hard."

"Wow, Sis. I didn't expect to see you."

"She insisted on coming to pick you up," Jeff said.

"And I'm glad she did." I let her down and looked at her. "I'm glad you did."

The whoosh of the baggage carousel began and the wiz and thud of the bags filled the air. We stood and looked at each other as we waited for my luggage.

"This is a great welcome home," I said. And then I shared a short conversation about the weather in Southern Ghana before my bags plopped down and started their ride around the silver merry-go-round.

Soon, we were parking, back at the small three-hundred-square-foot apartment that solidified my life back in reality.

That night, the three of us sat up for a short time, talking about my experiences in that other life—the life that was now both figuratively and literally, thousands of miles away. I asked my sister about school. She told me she would have her medical assistant certification in nine months. And then, I was dead to the world, travel, excitement, and jet lag catching up with me. When I woke in the morning, Jeff was snuggled next to me in our small bed and my sister was asleep on a small blow-up mattress just a few feet away, next to the kitchen. I barely remembered pulling out the bed and placing my head on the pillow the night before.

After we were all awake, we sat at the small table next to the kitchen and ate a quick meal consisting of coffee, toast, and boiled eggs. And then we walked my sister out to her car.

"Hey, sis. I'm glad you came to pick me up last night."

"Thanks. I love you."

"I love you, too." We hugged. "We'll make sure to see more of each other."

"Yeah. Let's plan on it."

"See you later, sweetie, " Jeff added as she climbed into her car and gave us a final wave.

Chapter Seventeen

It took me a full two weeks to get acclimated back into my old life, although I felt much different and had a newfound determination to move forward and make a difference. My focus now was on finding a job that gave me the same satisfaction I had teaching children in the village on the other side of the world. While Jeff was still working at the investment company, albeit in a new, permanent role, I wanted to continue serving, to keep giving of myself. What I didn't realize is, I was trying to replicate an experience that I would not find in my backyard. I was searching for the profound, immersive experience that was a half a world away. So, since I had bills to pay and life to live in my own reality, I found a job at a local youth center working with kids in an after-school program. It was okay for the time being—tutoring elementary students from a local school, helping with art programs, and open gym. I also spent two mornings a week volunteering at a food shelter, serving food or packing boxed lunches. It was a far cry from the village in Ghana, but it felt like good work.

On a rainy day in late October, I woke early. I sat up in bed and wiped my eyes. I was feeling a bit groggy as I had never been a morning person. I looked at my phone on the side table, still a half hour until Jeff's alarm would fill the air with the dreaded wake-up call. I sat on the side of the bed, stretched my hands to the ceiling, and set my feet on the fuzzy rug that shielded my feet from the cold floor. I felt my legs stretch as I made my way to the bathroom and stood in front of the toilet, filling the porcelain bowl with a deep gurgling splash.

I walked to the sink and washed my hands, but spent an extra thirty seconds staring at my puffy eyes, doing what I did many mornings, reliving memories of my days working in the village on the other side of the world, using the memories almost like a mantra—making sure I remembered, and never forgot, the work I did, the people I met.

I quietly walked to the kitchen, making sure not to disturb Jeff, allowing him the final twenty-seven minutes of respite before his day began. I started a pot of coffee and sat at the small table that housed two laptops and a few dirty glasses, listening to the bubbling drip of the coffee maker as the nutty aroma filled the room.

I situated myself in my seat and flipped open my laptop. I read through my news feed and was quickly turned off when three articles in a row were filled with nothing but anger and babble about politics. So, I clicked on my email icon and scrolled through my new messages, deleting a dozen or so unnecessary advertisements and pleads for campaign donations. That left six unopened emails, one of which caught my attention right off. It was from Don Alanson, one of my psychology professors. I hadn't heard from him since he returned my final paper which I told him was as much catharsis as it was research. Normally when papers were graded they were returned through the school portal and I would read the professor's comments online. With my last paper, Professor Alanson contacted me and asked me to meet with him to go over his review in person.

We spent forty-five minutes discussing it in depth and how moved by my work he was. He told me that the personal aspect added a depth that he had never come across before. He told me there was a realism that came from first-hand experience that was strengthened by well-documented research. In fact, he said, the portion about Christopher House was extremely poignant and was a perfect anecdote of the government's lack of funding to address homelessness.

I clicked on the email. It was short, just a few sentences. It started with a greeting and then, *Hope all is well since graduation. I am contacting you because I just had a conversation with a gentleman who is in charge of assigning grant money to nonprofits. I told him about the paper you wrote and he is interested in meeting with you. Give me a call.* He listed his number under his signature.

I looked at the clock on my computer and decided to wait a few hours before I called as the sun was barely showing itself over the horizon. I sat there wondering what he meant about grant money—about non-profits—and didn't see what that had to do with me. But I was intrigued.

I got up and quietly poured myself a cup of coffee and sat back at my computer. I pulled up the local newspaper online and read through the headlines—a few sports scores, an article about electric vehicles, and an op-ed about the upcoming gubernatorial election. I clicked on the next headline, "Homeless Encampment Cleared From Local Park," and just two paragraphs in, I shut my computer with a huff. My heart was pounding. Complaints from neighbors. The mayor and city council vowed to clean up the streets. *What the fuck?* I thought to myself. Where do they expect them to go? You sweep one area clean and another homeless village is erected in another part of the city. "It's not a solution," I said in a whisper. I sat there stewing in my thoughts when the buzz-buzz of Jeff's alarm made me jump. I looked over as he sat up on the edge of the bed.

"Morning," I said.

He turned toward me with a confused look. "What are you doing up?"

"Couldn't sleep."

"That's what you get for going to bed before nine." He yawned, stretched his arms, and walked to the bathroom.

"You want a cup of coffee?" I said with a raised voice.

"Yeah, sure," he called from the bathroom.

We sat together at the table, sipping our coffee and reading. I decided to forego the daily news for a novel that's been sitting next to my bed, a page dogeared halfway through, while Jeff sifted through the newsfeed on his phone. "Here's something interesting," he said, breaking the silence. "There's an art exhibit at the community center this Saturday. You up for going?" I shrugged. "Do you have plans?"

"No. Just not in the mood."

"Hmm—anything you want to talk about?"

I sat quietly for a moment and then opened my computer and turned it toward him, the article still on the screen. He paused and read and then looked at me with a crooked smile, and shook his head. "What're yuh thinking?"

I huffed and looked off in the distance. "I don't know." I picked up my coffee and took a drink. I could feel my brows furrow and a sense of frustration rose in my gut. "It feels so far away, like it has nothing to do with me anymore, but I won't let that happen. I want it to bother me. I want it to stir something up inside me."

"Okay. Is there something you want to do about it?"

"Yeah, but I'm still looking for the answer to that question."

"You know what it sounds like to me?"

"What?" I looked at him intently.

"It has something to do with you. It is part of you—the street will always be a part of you. You know how you told me you used to try and put your past behind you? You've actually done the exact opposite. You've embraced it. You have taken it on as part of who you are—and that's a good thing. Use that as a motivation. Use that as a reason to help. I see what you do. Your time in Ghana—your time with the after-school program—those are ways that you have chosen to embrace your understanding of your suffering, your hardships, and give back what you have learned—to serve others who are in similar circumstances to what you have experienced."

We sat in silence.

"I can't sit here and tell you I totally understand what you are feeling," he continued. "But what I can tell you is that I see you light up when you talk about what you do—when you talk about helping students learn to read or when you volunteer at the food shelter. I saw how much it meant to you to visit Nadine and the mission and the alley. You are passionate and much of that is because of the difficulties you have faced in life. Let your emotions—let your passion—guide you in the direction you want to go. If that means being angered or frustrated when you read that article, so be it."

I shook my head and pursed my lips. I looked at him and nodded. I took a deep breath and held it in. I let out the stale air and then breathed in and filled my lungs.

"You alright?" He reached over and put his hand on mine.

"Yeah. I'm fine. I just have a lot I want to do and sometimes

I don't know which way to go."

"I get it. And I would love to sit here all morning and talk, but I have to get ready for work."

"Don't worry. I have a feeling I'll be dealing with this for a long time," I let out a soft breathy laugh.

An hour later, I made the bed and pushed it back into its home inside the convertible couch. I was alone and the small apartment was silent. I sat down and set my laptop on my legs and opened my photo app. I pulled up the pictures I had taken in Ghana and let the images invoke memories and emotions. I know I was romanticizing the experience, it was anything but easy, but the struggles, the difficulties of the work, my illness, all made the experience more meaningful. I pictured the ceiling above my bed in the small room inside the home I shared with the strangers who traveled across the world with me and became family. The ceiling above my bed became a familiar scene as I recovered from my illness.

I saw my students running in the dirt field, plumes of dust rising behind their scampering feet as they chased after the ball and struggled to help it find its place in the makeshift goal we erected with stumps from fallen trees. I pictured my travel companions. I pictured my Ghanaian colleagues. I remembered dancing and singing as we celebrated at the "apontow ma yɛn adamfofa"—the "feast for our friendship." And then I put words to feelings. I spoke to myself out loud— "service—service to others—service to those in need—make a difference—serve to make a difference—make a difference through service." And that was it—my goal—my mantra—my words to live by. I will *make a difference through service.*

I opened a document and began typing freely. *I was abandoned by my parents because they didn't approve of me. I ended up on the street, but fought back and rose again. I owe it to myself, to my determination, but also to those who served me and helped me find my path once again. I will extend my hand. I will help others rise, get back on their feet, and find their path. I will remember my struggles. I will remember those who served me. I will make a difference through service.*

I read it out loud. I read it silently. I whispered it to myself one last time.

* * *

The phone rang several times and then a voice rang out on the other end, "Mr. Alanson speaking." I said hi and introduced myself, reminding him I was the student he emailed about the research paper.

"I'm glad you got my email. I've been thinking about your paper a lot lately." There was a slight pause. "In fact, it's been on my mind quite a bit. I'm still intrigued with the way you weaved personal experience with your research." I thanked him and we spent a few minutes talking about my experiences.

"So," he brought us back to the topic of his email. "I was talking with a friend of mine the other day who is in charge of awarding grants to nonprofits in the area. He was telling me about a grant that specifically supports programs working with marginalized populations and I immediately thought of your paper and about Christopher House. I have such a vivid picture of it in my mind from your description, I feel like I have a connection with it myself."

"Wow. I'm glad to hear that."

"And, anyway, he was interested in hearing more, so I forwarded him a copy of your paper. I hope that's okay."

"Yeah, of course, it's okay."

"Well, he wants to talk to you and Nadine is it?"

"Yeah, Nadine is the contact at Christopher House."

"I'm assuming you can help relay the information to her."

"Yes. I can do that—what's the grant for exactly?"

"I don't have all the specifics, but it has to do with funding mental health services and medical care through non-profits in the inner city. It sounds like it's specifically targeting the homeless, offering them counseling services, vaccines, and medical checkups. I'll forward you the information. The contact is Gerald Johnson. I gave him your name."

"I really appreciate it, Mr. Alanson."

"It's my pleasure. Your paper is an inspiration."

We talked for a few more minutes. I shared a bit about my Ghana experience. He told me it didn't surprise him that I would make such an amazing journey and then he asked if I would be interested in presenting my paper to one of his classes. I told him I would be honored.

After I hung up the phone, I took a minute to get my thoughts together and then called the number Mr. Alanson had given me. There was no answer, so I left a message and then sat there for a while letting everything sink in, and I decided I would wait until I talked to Mr. Johnson about the grant before I talked to Nadine.

That night while I was helping a fifth grader with his English homework, I got the feeling that something special was about to happen, that everything I had been doing in my life up until that point was driving me to a crossroads. The work I was doing at that exact moment seemed more important than it had before. For some reason, pitching a tent in the alley, passing out socks to the homeless while I was still technically homeless myself, focusing my studies on social and clinical psychology, volunteering my time in a third-world country, and working with kids in an after-school program, all seemed to be equally important, and all seemed to be pointing me in one direction. I was not quite sure where that direction was going to end up or where the crossroads would actually intersect, but after the conversation with my professor, I felt it was all coming together.

When I got home from work that night, Jeff was lying in our pull-out bed watching the news. I walked in with a bit more gusto than usual and Jeff sat up and turned my way. "Sounds like a freight train just entered the apartment."

"Sorry—didn't mean to disturb you."

"It's okay, but what's with all the energy this evening?"

"Just had a good day."

"Nice to hear—much better than how it started this morning, huh?"

"For sure." I took off my coat and hung it on the back of one of the chairs at the table next to the kitchen. I sat down, leaned over, and untied my shoes, and then rested my elbows on my knees. "I did get some interesting news after you left this morning." I sat up and looked at him. "I got an email from the psych professor who I did that last research paper for."

"What about?" He sat up straight and looked at me.

"He gave my paper to one of his friends who deals with grants for nonprofit organizations. He thinks Christopher House may qualify for one of the grants." Jeff nodded his head. "The guy wants to talk with me about it, so I called and left him a message."

He walked over and sat in a chair next to me. "That's cool."

"I don't really know much, except it's for work with the

homeless, something to do with mental health counseling and vaccines."

"Exciting. Now why don't you get ready for bed and cuddle up with me while I fall asleep? I have an early morning meeting."

"Not sure I can fall asleep yet, but I'll give it a try.

Half an hour later, I turned over and pulled the silver chain on the lamp next to my side of the bed—Jeff was lying, back to me, breathing heavily. I grabbed a book from the side table, flipped to the dog-eared page, and allowed myself to get lost in the story, trying to let the events of the day go so my mind and body could relax. But after about ten pages, I was still wide awake. I sat on the edge of the bed, thinking—my mind back on Mr. Alanson—anticipating the callback from the state's grants office, wondering what exactly the grant entailed.

I got up and found my spot at the small table next to the kitchen, laptop calling me, telling me to search, to find, to look for clues to what grant may be waiting on the other side of the anticipated phone call. I found a state website titled *Current Request for Grant Applications*. I scrolled through, searching for clues to a possible match. I spent forty-five minutes reading—scrolling, searching— scrolling—searching—reading—searching—reading—scrolling, and then finally, leaned back in my chair and stared at the ceiling, no closer to an answer than I was earlier in the day. I looked at the clock at the bottom of my screen. It was two a.m. and I was still wide awake. I sat back trying to figure out what to do next and decided to brave the cold October morning and walk to the corner store for a snack.

I bundled up in my winter Jacket, rummaged through the bottom drawer of my dresser for my scarf and gloves, and then, before walking out the door into the dark drizzle, I reached my hand into my backpack hanging on a hook on the wall, snagged my earphones and stuffed them in my ears.

I walked down the hall, down the stairs, and out the front door onto the stoop. I stood for a moment, tightened my scarf, zipped up my coat, and clicked on my favorite playlist. I stepped out into the darkness, felt a misty rain on my face, and let the music dance in my ears. I walked the three blocks to the corner store, keeping my eyes on the lights on the poles interspersed evenly at the beginning, middle, and then again at the beginning of each block, a safety habit I picked up from a seasoned vet while I lived on the streets. He taught me to pay attention to the dim light on the edges of the lighted circle that illuminated the ground. He said that is where danger lurks, just outside the light. And, it seemed to work. It kept me alert and I never ran into the lurking danger, maybe because I was alert, maybe because there was no lurking danger. Either way, I stayed vigilant and I stayed safe.

Cars passed as I walked, rooster tails spraying from the rear tires. Across from the store sat a small encampment of blue tarps barely visible behind a set of shrubs next to a tire shop. I made it a point to look at it each time I passed. It was one of the secret ways I kept my experience relevant in my life and it ensured that those who lived there were seen, at least by someone. I was always compelled to walk over, tap on one of the tarps, and say hi—to introduce myself—but I never did. I know how I felt when I was in their place. I know how it was to feel invisible, but I also knew I didn't want to be seen. I was embarrassed. Most of the time I wanted to stay hidden.

Today, though, as I walked out of the store, I had two bags in my hand. One contained a chocolate milk and a can of salted peanuts, my favorite late-night snack. The other, two

Gatorades and four protein bars. I sat on a bench by the double glass doors in the front of the corner store, safe from the falling rain. Music played softly in my head as I drank my chocolate milk and watched the condo of tarps across the street. The current song ended and serendipitously, a song I had recently added to my playlist filled the space between my ears.

I let the soft notes caress my mind and fill my body. I sang the words softly to myself as if I was telling my own story. The song, "You Will Be Found" by Sam Smith, expressed exactly what I wanted to speak to those behind the blue tarps on the other side of the road. My heart started to pound. My eyes welled and a single tear ran down my cheek. *"Cause when you don't feel strong enough to stand / You can reach, reach out your hand / And oh, someone will come running and I know they'll take you home."* The comforting voice continued calling me—continued compelling me—continued urging me on. *"Lift your head and look around / You will be found." The voice faded and the music trailed off.*

I hit pause, took out my headphones, and put them in my pocket. I allowed myself to fully experience the elements—the rain, the darkness, the soft wind. I stood and walked out from under cover, unzipping my coat, undoing my scarf, and feeling the cold night on my body. I took off my hat and let the rain soak my hair and roll down my face. *I* walked across the street and set the bag with the Gatorades and protein bars next to an opening in one of the blue tarps. I was compelled to say hello, but stood for a moment and then turned and walked slowly away, allowing my shirt under my open coat to soak up the rain—allowing the world to hover around me—to get close to me—so I would never forget.

* * *

My phone rang about half past nine. I turned over, groggy from my early morning excursion, and looked at the number on the screen. I didn't recognize it and was then jarred awake with the thought that it might be a call about the grant. I sat up quickly, took a shallow breath, touched the green button on the screen, and put the phone to my ear. "Hello?" I said, trying to sound as awake as possible. Then I reacted with, "Shoot," and an irritated shake of my head as the person on the other end tried to get me to upgrade my cell phone plan. "No thanks." I hung up and plopped my head back on my pillow. But I couldn't fall back asleep as the dim light protruded weakly through cloud cover, bounced through the crack in the curtains, and landed squarely on my face.

I stayed in bed for another thirty minutes, wanting to get up and close the crack in the curtains, but too tired to make the effort. I pulled the cover tight to my chin and turned away from the window, but eventually sat up in somewhat of a sleepy daze. I got up and walked over to the fridge, opened the door, and pulled out the half-full chocolate milk from my trip to the corner store. I lifted it to my lips, tilted my head back, and let the cool liquid fill my mouth, flow down my throat, and coat my stomach.

I looked over at the small table by the kitchen. Next to my laptop sat the open peanut container I munched on briefly before heading to bed a few hours ago. I leaned over, filled my hands, and then my mouth, letting my tongue ingest the salty morsels. I picked up my phone, connected it to a small Bluetooth speaker on the far side of the three-hundred-square-foot apartment, and then listened to soft sounds fill the air. I sat, allowing myself to wake to the day, knowing I didn't have work until late afternoon, as the melodious sounds flowed in and out of my mind along with thoughts of the misty night and the blue tarps. I enjoyed working late in the day because I enjoyed slow mornings—because I enjoyed my time alone, my time gathering my thoughts as the sun popped its head up above the horizon and eventually found its peak high above the clouds. It gave me time to wake up. It gave me time to pop my head up and find my peak. And that's what I did that morning. I relaxed at the small table and filled my mouth with peanuts several times, gazed into nothingness, and listened to soft jazz.

Eventually, I got up, made a cup of coffee, folded the blankets on the bed, and transformed the bed back to a couch so I could lounge a bit longer, stretching out with a book, head on the armrest on one end, feet crossed on top of the armrest on the other. I found the dog-eared page halfway through the book and read, the music continuing to play in the background.

I was re-reading a book I had read in high school. Jeff and I were browsing through a used book store downtown a couple weeks before and I came across an old beige copy of *Fahrenheit 451*. I always remembered enjoying it, even though I felt like some of the deeper concepts flew over my head at the time. I thumbed through the pages, stopping every once in a while to read a paragraph or two, somewhat searching for a message I vaguely remembered my teacher pinpointing in the story. And all of a sudden, there it was. I was carried back in time, to eleventh grade. I could see my English teacher walking around the room, book in hand, waving his arms, asking questions, highlighting the author's words, explaining the author's message. I was mesmerized as I read, "Everyone must leave something behind when he dies... Something your hand touched some way so your soul has somewhere to go when you die... It doesn't matter what you do... so long as you change something from the way it was before you touched it into something that's like you after you take your hands away." I stopped reading. I stood. I looked off into nothing, my mind stuck on those words, "...Change something from the way it was before you touched it into something that's like you after you take your hands away." My mind wandered through memories. I asked myself—What have I touched? What have I changed? I thought about Ghana. I thought about the children at the after-school program. I searched my heart and I knew I had to do more. I had to find ways to make a difference—a lasting difference. I had to find ways to change things, to help people, to influence lives. I walked to the front counter and purchased the book.

Still lying on the couch, halfway through the Novel that had unknowingly sat in my subconscious for years, my phone rang again. This time, I didn't answer. I was at an intense part of the book and didn't want to put it down. I let my phone ring as I continued to read, and then, less than a minute after the ringing stopped, a soft ping emitted from my phone. I read to the end of the page, turned the top corner down to save my spot, and set the book on the armrest of the couch. I picked up my phone and listened to the message. *Hello. This is Gerald Johnson. I'm returning your call about a grant opportunity. I will be around my phone most of the day, but do have a lunch meeting between eleven-thirty and one. I look forward to speaking with you.*

I listened to the message a second time and sat there, anticipation growing. *Should I call back right away? Should I wait a little while?* I wondered, not wanting to look too anxious. I checked the time—eleven o'clock, and picked up the phone not wanting to wait until he returned from lunch.

"Hello, Gerald Johnson speaking."

I introduced myself and connected my inquiry with Professor Alanson.

"Yes. I have your paper sitting on my desk—very intriguing—well done."

"Thanks—so, Mr. Alanson said Christopher House might be a good fit for one of the grants your department is offering."

"Right. It seems to check all the necessary boxes. I was familiar with the organization, but did do some research after I read your paper and Christopher House seems to be a good fit." He paused for a moment. I wasn't sure if he was waiting for a response, so I remained silent. "This is one of our biggest grants." He continued. It is a two-year funding window from June 1 to June 1. It's called the Health and Welfare Grant. It covers both the mental and physical health of the homeless or others in disenfranchised or marginalized populations."

I tried to remain calm, but was genuinely excited. "That sounds like a great opportunity," I said energetically.

"It's a chance to provide a very needed service to a highly underserved population."

I dug for a bit more information. "So, if Christopher House receives the grant, what will they be doing exactly?"

"First, we will narrow down the applications to the top three to four candidates and then do site visits. One of the big requirements is the capacity to house a mental health counselor and a small medical staff of two to three nurses or physician assistants."

"Man—sounds like a substantial operation."

"For small organizations like Christopher House, it is substantial. That's why we need to ensure they are well-prepared, in terms of physical building space, staffing, and budget. Although the grant supplies the necessary revenue streams, if the program is not set up efficiently, there could be unforeseen expenses that divert money away from the organization's normal operating budget."

"Wooph—" I breathed out and then in again. "Sounds like a lot of work."

"It is—but as long as Christopher House has the basic requirements, we can supply the guidance needed—and the end game is worth it."

"What do I need to do?"

"I'd like you to be the go-between—the connection between Christopher House and my department. I'm not saying Christopher House has the grant, but if the right work is done, it has a great shot. We've had less than stellar results the two other times we tried to implement the program. One of the things we were lacking was one person who could make connections between the organization and my department—someone who could deliver and interpret information between the two entities—someone who could be proactive and deal with issues before they happen or at least before they become too big of an issue. It's easy to get overwhelmed if you don't have the right people in place."

"Hmmm—" I began feeling anxious—a combination of excitement and trepidation forming little bubbles in my stomach.

"I know this sounds like a lot—and it can be if you're not up for it. But I can walk you through everything." He gave me time to let it sink in. "Am I asking too much?" he finally inquired, his voice radiating a trustworthiness, a genuine caring. Yet I still had questions.

"I don't think so. I don't want it to be." I thought for a

moment. "What is my obligation? What is my actual role in this?"

"Your position will be vital, but unofficial. If the grant is secured, Nadine Peters and Pastor Jim—he searched for the correct surname—Pastor Jim Chambers will hire the people involved in direct service and supervision. There will be three to four front-line staff, a mental health counselor, and medical staff who can treat simple colds and infections, and administer vaccines. And then one supervisory position to manage the day-to-day operations and budget."

"I didn't see this coming," I told him. "When I talked to Professor Alanson initially, I thought it would be just a bit of money to support the programs they were already doing, but now I can tell it's quite a bit more than that."

"It's a decent undertaking, I'll give you that."

I laughed quietly and took a deep breath. "Yeah—well—how do we start?"

"I'll send you a link to the application. You've got about a month and a half until the deadline. It's due December 15. You need to meet with the people at Christopher House first. If they agree to give this a go, fill out as much of the application as you can. Do this before the Thanksgiving break and then forward it to me. That will give us a little over two weeks to finish everything up. I'll go over the initial paperwork and then we can set up a meeting to fill in the blanks and I can answer any questions that you guys have at that time."

"Okay—I can do that."

"And, don't hesitate to contact me in the meantime if you have pressing questions or if you get stuck on anything."

"Yeah—I will—and I'll call Nadine when I get off the phone."

"Great. I look forward to hearing from you soon."

I hung up the phone and sat there with a soft smile on my face, a feeling of both wonderment and bewilderment sat at the base of my throat, circling about, intermingling, not allowing me to know if I was excited or overwhelmed. I did know, though, that I was alive and that I was ready to move forward.

When I told Nadine about the grant and that the opportunity emerged from the research paper I interviewed her for, she was excited. I explained the general requirements for building space and the hiring and supervision of staff, at least as much as I could. We set an appointment to meet with Pastor Jim on Monday of the following week. She said she felt they had the space if they moved a few things around, but that we could talk more in-depth when we met. She helped me create a username and password for the online documents and I shared the link with her. She told me she and Pastor Jim would read through the documents before Monday. "Thanks for all your help," she said. "You're a blessing."

After I got off the phone, I was so excited I texted Jeff, "Big news about the grant. Got to go to work soon. Let's go to that art exhibit this weekend." I watched three dots flash at the bottom of the text, dot-dot-dot, dot-dot-dot, dot-dot-dot.

"Excited to hear details. Yes, art exhibit on Sat..."

* * *

On Saturday, I woke to a warm pot of coffee brewing in our small kitchen. The aroma seemed to be dancing in the air, bouncing off the walls, calling me to wake. I opened one eye halfway to see Jeff at the stove, steam rising from a pan. I heard the crack of an egg and the sizzle that followed as it oozed onto the hot surface. A few moments later he laid four strips of bacon down to cook and quickly the coffee merged with the overactive amino acids of the fatty breakfast staple. I opened both eyes and sat up. "Okay—if you're trying to torture me awake, you've done your job."

He looked at me and cracked a smile, "Not my intention, but the perfect residual effects of a good breakfast."

I walked over to him in the kitchen and put my arm around his shoulder. "If we're going to spend the day in town, I'll need a full belly."

"Take a seat and relax. Your waiter will serve you soon." He turned and gave me a quick, yet intimate kiss on the mouth. I smiled, slapped him on the rear end, and took my seat at the small table next to the kitchen.

"What's this exhibit about today, anyway?" I asked as I waited patiently for my food.

"Sounds like a combination of a few different local artists. Some photography, I think. Some watercolor and oil paintings. And, I think one of the guys works in wood mediums." He walked over and set a plate in front of me. "Your meal is served." He bowed his head at me and then looked up and winked. "I talked with one of my colleagues about the show and he says one of his cousins will have some of her work there. Sounds like she is a pretty well-known painter. I think he said she works with oil paints."

I turned my phone over and looked at the screen. "What time do you want to leave?"

"Around nine should be fine."

"Nice. I can jump back in bed for thirty minutes before I start getting ready."

"Only if you let me join you," he said playfully from the other side of the table.

* * *

It was an unusually dry end to the month, but it had been raining off and on for the last couple weeks so the sense of moisture was still palpable as we walked the four blocks from our car to the exhibit. Today, the sky was clear and the sun shone bright in the crisp, fall sky. I looked up and watched a seagull glide to the ground and rummage through a small pile of garbage in the gutter just ahead of us. And then Jeff called my attention to a sign outside a group of apartments. "You wanna check this out first?" He pointed to a sandwich board that read, *Studios, One, & Two Bedrooms, Bay View, Now Leasing.*

"You got something in mind? I'm kinda partial to our intimate space."

"Just for fun. You never know."

"I do know we won't find our current rent at this place."

"I'm not worried. With my new job, we can afford to treat ourselves a bit nicer."

"It won't hurt to look, I guess. Once we find out how much these places cost I can always mourn when we get home." I giggled, but shot Jeff a menacing look to show him I was only half joking.

We walked into a foyer that housed a small table to the right and a bulletin board on the adjacent wall. The table contained a tray of cookies, crackers and cheese, and baby carrots flanked on either side by a large pot of freshly brewed coffee and a few bottled waters. We walked over to the bulletin board and read the notice about lease options, rent and move-in costs, and lease incentives.

"Huh—not as bad as I thought," I commented.

"And this is a cute entrance. Nice and clean—spacious," he

shot me a mischievous glance.

We walked straight ahead and through an open glass door over which hung a sign, *Leasing Office*, and found two young women sitting at desks on opposite sides of the room.

"Good afternoon," said the young woman on the right. "How may we help you?"

"We'd like to look at an apartment," Jeff said, and then looked at me, "One bedroom, maybe two."

"Okay. Why don't you take a seat and I'll show you what's available." We sat down in the chairs in front of her desk as she pecked away at her keyboard. "Alright, it looks like we have two, two-bedrooms and one, one-bedroom available. The rest are studios." She turned her computer screen toward us. "Here's the details. We're having a special right now—half off move-in costs, plus half off first month's rent." We looked at the screen and read silently.

"What do you think?" Jeff asked me.

"What's the difference between the two-bedroom apartments—the smaller one is a hundred and fifty dollars more a month?" I inquired, directing my question to the young woman.

She explained that the smaller apartment was on the back side of the building with less street noise and had a bay view. "You pay for a bit of luxury," She smiled and then offered to take us on a tour, dangling a key card in front of us.

We followed her to the elevator and watched her slide the key card into a slot. "You get added security here. Something you don't usually find at this price." She smiled sweetly as we stepped into the elevator.

The door slid open a few floors up. She led us down the hallway to the last door on the right, describing the amenities along the way—a covered barbecue area overlooking the water, a fitness center, and one off-street parking spot. She entered a code on the keypad and the deadbolt released with an electronic swoosh. She opened the door and invited us to enter ahead of her. We were met with a view through a wall of windows at the far end of the living room—the dimly lit blue sky and apartment buildings across the alley gave the illusion that the apartment was directly connected with the outside world. It was a stately manner compared to what we were used to—it was clean—it was spacious—it had two adequately sized bedrooms on either side of the bathroom on the left. There was a stackable washer and dryer, a nice kitchen and dining area, opening to a spacious living room on the right.

We slid the glass door open and stepped onto the small balcony. We looked at each other and said simultaneously, "Bay view?" and then laughed.

"Well, technically—" Our guide tried to sound convincing as she pointed between the buildings "—it's all yours."

"Yup—there it is," I said, winking at Jeff.

"And it could be ours," he replied, grabbing my hand and giving it a soft squeeze.

We checked out an apartment on the fourth floor and then one on the third. Both offered a lot more space than what we currently had and we agreed the idea of moving was enticing.

We made our way back outside and walked the final few blocks to the exhibit. It was surprisingly busy—groups of people walking about the displays, energetically discussing the different works. A buzz of interest was palpable. We were pleasantly surprised, as we were expecting a small, more quiet, intimate affair. We ended up buying an oil painting of three Indigenous fishing boats in the waters off the coast just a couple hours from the city. "I love it, but I'm not sure where we're going to put it," I said, as we carried the twenty-four by thirty-five-inch treasure around the remaining exhibits, the first significant purchase we'd made together.

"We can hang it in our new apartment," Jeff replied.

"Oh, our new apartment?" I raised my eyebrows and nodded.

"Yeah, got to buy classy art for our new place."

"Interesting—okay—yeah—in our new place." I smiled and put my hand on his shoulder.

We looked at some wood carvings, and then some watercolors, and then a small set of steel and wood sculptures, one of which we were compelled to buy, until we saw the price.

By the time we walked back outside, it was well past lunchtime. So, on our way to the car we searched for a restaurant. We decided on a small bar that I had heard good things about. It was a contemporary, industrial motif with exposed pipes and large Edison bulbs hanging in clusters about the ceiling and over the tables. We sat at a bar-height table with four chairs. There were several other small groups and couples sitting about the room. The air was full of clinking glasses, soft rock, and the bar's specialty, hot wings and sweet potato fries. While the ambiance was lively, it was calm and quiet enough for good conversation to happen organically.

We ordered the day's special, our choice of a microbrew from one of the many local distilleries and a dozen wings. We sat and waited for our food as we drank our malted refreshments and got a refill when the main course arrived. A few minutes later we were surprised by a friend of Jeff's who walked in with a woman he didn't recognize. He introduced himself as Jeremy, and his fiancée, Beth. Jeff invited them to join us. They sat and ordered the special. Jeff told us the story of their meeting a little over a year ago as "wet behind the ears errand boys," at their current firm. They were the only two interns who were offered permanent positions after the summer program ended.

We ended up staying and talking for a while, then walked to the back of the bar and played a couple games of pool. Outside of work, Jeremy and I had a lot in common. We both grew up playing sports, quarterbacked the high school football team, and played baseball. He minored in psychology and almost decided to pursue clinical psychology, but found he was more skilled with numbers and went into financing instead. We had a good conversation about the state of the social service industry and I started babbling about the lack of funding and then caught myself before getting too revved up. Beth was a sophomore in college, a music major thinking about going into teaching. "She's good enough," Jeremy made sure to add, "to make music her profession. She's currently in the city's Philharmonic Orchestra and has been asked to tour with them this spring and summer."

As we finished a second game of pool, they invited us to a party at a friend's condo downtown. "It's a casual dinner party," Jeremy told us, "maybe thirty or forty people. A bunch of intellectuals. Not really my crowd, but I went to high school with the guy." He shrugged. "His parents were pretty well off and he's connected with some people in some of the big tech companies around here. It's always fun to see who shows up— usually some big wig from a billion-dollar company that you never thought you would see in real life. It's worth going for the off chance."

Beth leaned over to us and smiled, "If nothing else, the food is usually amazing and the view is spectacular."

The party didn't start until seven, so we headed back home to drop off our artwork and change, then shared a Lyft with

Jeremy and Beth to a fifteen-story highrise clad in reflective glass. We checked in with the doorman, took the elevator to the twelfth floor, and found the condo at the end of a wide hallway. We knocked on door 1202 and a tall man in a pair of khakis rolled up above brown Chelsea boots, and a long-sleeved Henley top, opened the door and greeted us with a big smile. "Jeremy, Beth—glad you made it." We walked in and were immediately hit with a stunning view of the city from two walls of floor-to-ceiling windows that met at the corner of the expansive living room. Jeremy introduced us around the party and we snacked from plates of lavishly prepared cheeses, meats, and crackers, and sipped on what I assumed was some expensive wine—although I wouldn't have known the difference.

Over the next forty-five minutes, the room filled with people, a soft beat played in the background, side conversations commenced, and dinner was served buffet style. At first, we found ourselves off in a corner making our own conversation, much of which revolved around comments about the artwork on the walls, the size of the bathroom, and what giant corporation we thought each new person who walked through the door was affiliated with. But as the night progressed, we found our way into a few conversations with others as people sat casually around the room on chairs, on the floor, at the bar looking into the kitchen eating chicken, prime rib, and salad. At one point, Jeremy introduced us to Kim and Hector, a couple who lived about thirty minutes away and owned an advertising agency. Jeremy told us that Kim spent time volunteering at a couple different community agencies and we would probably have a lot to talk about. One of the agencies she spent time at was a few blocks from Christopher House. It was an organization focused on finding homes for children who went undetected by the foster care system. They called them the lost children. The organization's main goal was to find the children a bed and a safe, temporary place to stay while they registered them with foster care or found relatives willing to take them in.

I told her about my connection to Christopher House and the grant we're applying for. She showed interest and told me that, each year, in addition to volunteering, she and her husband choose one or two non-profit organizations to donate a portion of the net profits from their business. "The amount is always different," she said, "depending on how much money we bring in each year." She handed me her card and smiled. "If you ever need anything."

We shared some stories about our experiences working with the homeless, she with children as young as three, me mainly with teens and adults, but a few families with kids, as well. Our eyes welled with tears. But, we ended the night with a few laughs, as Hector broke into the conversation and asked how Jeff and I met. "We knew each other for a while," I told them, "but we ran into each other at a coffee shop one day. The next day we ended up going on an odd, but sort of sweet road trip on Jeff's bike," I explained. Jeff swore it was more romantic than it sounded. "Sure," I chuckled, "I was sitting on the back of your bike hanging on for dear life, wondering where in the world we were going."

Jeff put his hand on my shoulder, "It must have worked, though," he winked at me.

Hector said that Kim was drawn to his charm and his Greek accent when they met at a conference about fifteen years ago. "She couldn't resist my charm."

Kim looked at him with a sideways grin. "Really, I felt sorry for him after he wouldn't stop calling me." She put her arm around his waist. "So I gave in and went out with him." She tilted her head back and laughed and then kissed him on the cheek. He put his arm around her shoulders and pulled her close. They looked at each other briefly, but in a way that communicated their connection, in a way I had not seen adults look at each other before.

I looked at them, twenty years our senior, and wondered where Jeff and I would be at their age. Hector and Kim displayed a much different relationship than I experienced growing up. My parents rarely showed affection in our own home, let alone in public. My parents went to church and claimed a Christian life—whatever that means—and would announce to those they talked to that everything was God's will or they would quote scripture when they didn't like what someone else was doing or how they were living their lives. But they never experienced much outside their church, their limited sphere of influence, and they never helped others or extended a hand to those in need if it wasn't directly connected to that small sphere. Conversely, Hector and Kim went out of their way to make a difference in other people's lives without preaching, without proclaiming God's plan. Maybe they believed in God—maybe not. No matter. I was drawn to their passion for each other and their unceremonious passion for service to their community and the people in it. I was drawn to their matter-of-factness— to the simplicity of what they did. They did what they did because people needed help—people needed support.

I took a mental picture—Hector, his arm around Kim, smile on both their faces—and saved it for reference.

Chapter Eighteen

On Monday, I woke early—excited to meet with Nadine and Pastor Jim—excited to finalize the paperwork for the grant. Normally I would wait for the bus outside our apartment, take the thirty-minute ride into town, and then walk a block to my destination. Today, I decided to take a Lyft, a lavish expense I usually saved for special occasions, like the party on Saturday night. But, in my mind, this was a special occasion, as well.

When I arrived at Christopher House, I was unusually nervous. I felt a buzz of excitement in my stomach and my hands were shaking. I took a deep breath and walked around the block before going inside. I wasn't sure exactly why my emotions were out of whack, but, nonetheless, I was able to walk in relatively composed.

Pastor and Nadine were sitting at a small table by the far wall. They each had a laptop and what appeared to be a cup of coffee in front of them. They stood up and greeted me and then offered me a seat on a set of small couches in the middle of the room. We sat facing each other getting caught up and sharing a few memories. "So, this is a big opportunity you've found for us," Pastor Jim said when our conversation slowed. "We really appreciate what you're doing."

"Oh—well—thanks, but it really wasn't me. My professor

is the one who hooked us up with Mr. Johnson at the grants office."

"Yes, but you're putting in the time—and it was your paper that got it all going."

"It's the least I can do. You guys did so much for me—you do so much for people."

"Well, anyway," Nadine smiled and put her hand on mine, "Thanks."

We moved over to the table and pulled up the application on Pastor's computer. He placed the laptop in the middle and we huddled around it. He and Nadine had already answered most of the questions and highlighted a few that they needed further information for. We did a little research, discussed a few thoughts and ideas, and filled out two more questions together. One of the remaining questions addressed the space needed to run the program. I could tell they were both hopefully optimistic, but also knew this was the one spot that could trip up the application.

We went to the back room and talked about what we thought should be done to make the space work. At minimum, they would have to clear out two decent-sized storage rooms to open up space for the counseling office and medical room. Even then, neither had windows and were both just barely big enough. And, they needed to find a place to store the supplies.

"Don't worry," I told them, "We have time to figure that part out. The application is due December 15 and they won't do site visits for a couple months." I looked around the room. "Let's just describe what is possible with the space you have, not worrying what it will actually take to get it where we need it."

"Yup—okay—let's do it," Pastor said with conviction. "With

your enthusiasm and God's grace, I'm sure it will come to-gether." He reached over and patted me on the back.

We went back to the front room, finished filling out the forms, and submitted the application. We looked at each other for a moment. "It's in God's hands," Nadine said.

"I've got to go to work, but I'll keep in touch." They walked me out to the front of the building. Nadine gave me a hug. Pastor put his hand on my shoulder and took a deep breath. "I'm gonna take on as much of the extra work as I can," I said, trying to build my own confidence as much as I was trying to reassure them.

"We know," Pastor said, "and we're grateful for all your help."

I showed up a half an hour early to the after-school program and sat there, running ideas through my head, thinking about how to make it all come together—the needed space, the money it would take to transform the dark, dingy storage rooms into spaces that meet the needs of the program. I wasn't quite sure how we were going to make it come together, but I told myself I would rack my brain trying to figure it out.

* * *

The Christmas season was over and New Year's was a few weeks gone. We had a stack of unfolded boxes on the small table next to the kitchen in our soon-to-be former apartment, waiting to be filled and trucked a few miles into town, up to the sixth floor, and into their new home—our new home. We decided to "bite the bullet" as Jeff put it and begin our new life, close to, but not quite in the heart of the city, but within walking distance of everything the city had to offer.

Jeff had just left for work and it was my goal to begin sorting through our things and getting the packing started. I moved the boxes to the unmade bed and sat at the table with my morning coffee, determined to allow myself time to wake up before diving into the task at hand. I sipped my coffee and opened my laptop. I cruised through my daily newsfeed, not finding anything that caught my attention, and then opened my email.

Delete. Delete. Delete. I cleared out my inbox until I came across an email from Gerald Johnson, titled, Site Visit, addressed to all three of us—Pastor Jim, Nadine, and me. My heart pounded as I clicked on the link. *Christopher House has been selected as one of three finalists for the Health and Welfare Grant. We would like to set up an appointment to complete a site visit within the next two weeks.* There were instructions to fill out the attached document and Gerald's digital signature at the bottom.

I immediately picked up my phone and called Nadine. Before she could say hello, I started talking a hundred miles an hour.

"Whoa... hold on a second," she interrupted me and asked me to slow down.

I took a breath. "Did you see the email about the grant that came in this morning?"

"Yes. I just read it a couple minutes ago. I'll go over it with Pastor when he gets here in the next hour."

"Great—let me know when you set the appointment so I can put it on my schedule."

"We'll make sure to let you know," she reassured me.

"And we should probably have a meeting beforehand to go over how to present the space," I added, trying to sound calm.

"Yeah, we'll make sure to do that. I'll fill out the form with Pastor and then we'll call you."

I got off the phone a little perplexed and sat for a few minutes mulling over our conversation. Something in Nadine's voice was off—a bit of uncertainty maybe—and then I put it out of mind as I sorted through drawers of kitchen utensils, pots and pans, and packed boxes the rest of the morning. When I got to work, I tried to focus on seventh-grade math as I helped a young boy struggling to convert fractions to decimals, all along, my mind running in circles.

The next day, while I continued my foray through the cluttered apartment—packing, taping, and filling boxes—Nadine called and gave me the date for the site visit. "We have a little over a week to meet and figure out how to make this work," she said, sounding a bit better today, but still not completely dispelling my anxiety.

When I arrived at Christopher House two days later, no one was in the waiting room, but I found Nadine, Pastor Jim, and a contractor in the back discussing needed upgrades to the facilities. Pastor introduced me to the contractor and had him explain what needed to be done. It wasn't as simple as moving the supplies from the storage closets and replacing it with a couple tables and chairs. The square footage had to be expanded, the lights and wiring needed to be upgraded to code, and one egress window needed to be installed in each room. Along with that, the bunk rooms on the other side needed to be brought up to code as well. If Christopher House was to be awarded the grant, officials had to be convinced that the back half of the building would be ready to pass inspection on time. We had to come up with a plan. We had to figure out how we were going to find funding for the renovation.

"Here's the quote for all the work," Pastor handed me a slip of paper filled with numbers.

I scanned down to the bottom of the page and let out an audible laugh. "That's quite a number."

"Yeah—so we've been discussing options," Pastor smirked.

"What've you come up with?"

"We've called in a few favors and have come up with about half."

"Okay—that's a start," I said optimistically.

"It is, but we need to find a solution to present to the city during the site visit."

"Yeah—right—well, we still have a few days."

"And we'll keep racking our brains," Nadine added.

"We're going to have to find a donor," Pastor clarified.

We stood there for a bit, discussing the scope of the work and bouncing ideas off each other. But nothing seemed to stick.

"Wait," I said suddenly. They looked at me. "Hold on a minute—I have an idea." I pulled my wallet out and shuffled through the contents. "Ahh—yeah—here it is," I said, emitting a satisfying breath.

"What's up?" Pastor asked.

"I'll be right back. I'm gonna make a phone call." I walked out to the waiting room. I pulled out my cell phone, dialed the number on the business card Kim gave me at the party a few weeks ago, and then sat and waited for it to ring.

"Hello?" A soft voice answered. I returned the greeting and reminded her who I was. "Oh, yes—from the party. How're you doing?"

I explained the situation and was surprised at how much she knew about Christopher House and how much she remembered about the grant I told her about at the party. She asked me several questions and told me she would make a few calls. "Give me forty-eight hours. I'll let you know what I come up with."

A little over forty-eight hours later I was at Christopher House with Nadine, Pastor, and their contractor, preparing for a meeting with Kim when the front door opened and she walked in with her husband Hector and an entourage of contractors and business owners. I stood up and met them in the middle of the waiting room. Anticipating a meeting with Kim, I was surprised at the size of her group. I introduced our team to hers. A round of handshakes ensued and we headed to the back room to look over the facilities.

The meeting began and ended in just under ninety minutes. There was no small talk—everyone knew why they were there and knew the urgency. After touring the facilities, the contractors pulled out a few small tools and dug in a bit deeper, evaluating and discussing the scope of the work. Kim and Hector sat down with Nadine and Pastor Jim. They went over logistics, timelines, and funding. Kim and Hector brought with them two friends who owned relatively large companies in the city. They were known for funding projects for small startups and nonprofits and were interested in supporting Christopher House.

When the contractors were done, they gave a revised work order and budget to the group. All three contractors would be donating their labor which helped significantly. And with a six-week timeline, the work would be done well ahead of schedule. Now it was up to Nadine and Pastor Jim to put together a proposal to hand to city officials on the day of the walk-through.

When the meeting was over, there was an air of optimism and Nadine and Pastor were noticeably relaxed. Nadine promised to keep everyone up to date on the status of the proposal and the impending grant decision. Before she left, Kim turned to me and smiled, "We got your back. Everything is in place."

I returned the smile, "Thanks, Kim. Thanks, Hector. I'm at a loss for words. You guys are amazing."

"We do what we can. Talk to you soon," Hector reached out his hand and we shook.

Kim gave me a hug, looked at me, and said in a quiet voice, "You're doing a great job."

After everyone was gone, Pastor brought out three bottled waters and we sat on the couches in the middle of the waiting room letting everything soak in. Few words were said, but the feeling of relief was clear.

I looked at Nadine and then at Pastor, smiles resting peacefully on their faces. I pulled my phone out and looked at the time. "I hate to leave, but I have work in a little bit," I said, breaking the relaxed silence. They both looked at me, appearing to be in deep thought.

Nadine shook her head. "I'm having a hard time wrapping my head around what just happened. I've never experienced anything like it."

"It's like an army of angels came out of thin air," Pastor added. "Where did you meet them?"

"I met Kim and Hector at a dinner party a few weeks ago. A friend of Jeff introduced us."

"Well, it was divine intervention. Thanks be to God," Pastor held his hand in the air."

"Amen," Nadine and I said in unison.

Eight days later, Nadine called me. "We just finished the site visit. They seemed impressed with the renovation proposal and it sounds like the community support could be the tipping point if the grant goes our way."

"Nice—I'm excited. When do you think you'll hear back?"

"They have one more visit this week and they'll be making a final decision within ten days."

The next two weeks went painstakingly slow, but finally, at nine a.m., two Tuesdays after the site visit, Nadine called. It was official. I was sitting at the table in our new apartment, no longer next to the tiny kitchen in the cramped three-hundred-square-feet, but a table built for four, next to what we felt was a kitchen built for royalty. She greeted me with a joyful tone. "Hey there. We got the news," she sang through the phone.

"Okay—what's the word?" I said with trepidation.

"We got it. Christopher House is the recipient of the Health and Welfare Grant." I could feel her smile through the receiver.

I leaned my head back and let out a guttural laugh toward the ceiling—heart pounding—lungs heaving in and out. Finally, I was able to manage a quick, "Wow—amazing."

"Yes it is," Nadine replied. "We have a lot of planning to do. We'll be getting an email in the next couple of days with a timeline and instructions for the next step."

"Doesn't seem real."

"Real or not, we need to buckle up for some work."

"Yeah—sounds like it," I replied, head reeling with disbelief.

"We'd like to have a little celebration and go over the logistics next week. Are you free to meet next Tuesday at ten?"

"I'll make sure I am."

"Great—see you soon."

* * *

When I walked into Christopher House I figured there would be a bit of fanfare as Nadine said they wanted to celebrate, yet I was the only one in the waiting room when I entered. I went to the back room to see if anyone was there, but it was empty, not just of people, but it had been cleared out of its normal clutter, as well. I checked my phone. It was a few minutes before ten. I had no phone calls or texts. I sat down at the table and waited. Finally, the door to the back room opened and Pastor appeared, a computer bag in one hand and a coffee in the other. "Hey there," he greeted me with a smile.

I stood up. "Hey, Pastor."

"Go ahead and take a seat. I thought we could go over the timeline and I can give you a few details while we wait for Nadine. She'll be here in a few minutes."

I sat back down and Pastor set a stack of papers on the table. He pulled a chair close to me and sat down. "So," he began, "we've got a lot to do before we open this new program in June." He thumbed through the paperwork, pulled out a green sheet with a list of dates, and set it on top of the stack. "This is our target date—June 15 is the day we plan to open the doors. Everything else leads up to the grand opening." He ran his finger down the line of dates and highlighted a number of key points that he said are "measuring sticks for our progress." He told me about finalizing paperwork, starting construction, and hiring staff.

The front door opened and Nadine walked in. "I made it guys. Hope you didn't get too far without me."

"I was just going over the schedule with him. You made it just in time."

"Just in time for what?" I asked.

"Nadine and I wanted to talk with you about something."

"Yes, we do," She sat down next to me. "We want you to be a part of all this. This is as much your program as it is ours."

"Of course. I'm going to do whatever I can."

Pastor turned his laptop toward me. "We want you to be an official part of the program." He pointed to the heading, *Clinical Psychology Certification*. "It's six months. Starting in May."

I looked at the screen. And then at Pastor.

"None of this would be possible without you." Nadine reached out and put her hand on my shoulder. "We'd like you to start as a half-time program director while you take evening classes."

I looked at the screen and read, my stomach churning with excitement. "Huh?" I sat silently for a few seconds. "I never thought about this before."

"You mean about becoming a counselor?" Pastor asked.

"Yeah—it just never crossed my mind."

"We think you'd be perfect. You have the education, but most of all, you have the life experience. You can relate to the people who would be seeking your help."

I leaned back in my chair.

"We would hire another psychologist to start," he explained. "In fact, we have someone in mind—someone who would be a good mentor to you." They both looked at me. "So, we thought you could start as a part-time director and then after you get your certification, you would come on full-time and split the director and counseling duties with Allison, the other psychologist."

"Have you talked to her about it?"

"Yeah—talked to her a couple days ago. She's a good person. I think you guys will get along well." Pastor stood up. "Come here for a second." The three of us walked to the back room. "Picture this place, after the renovation, two huge rooms with light streaming in from the new windows, and a reception desk in between. One is the counseling office—the other is a medical room for the nurses. It's all scheduled to be done in mid-May," We stood there visualizing the new setup.

"So?" Nadine calked her head and looked at me. "What do you think?"

I shook my head in disbelief. "What can I say?" I walked in a small circle, taking it all in. "I love you guys." I stood for a moment longer. "Yeah—of course I'll do it." We all erupted in laughter. A feeling of complete joy overtook me. I had never felt this level of happiness before. We hugged and my eyes filled with tears.

Nadine went over to the fridge on the other side of the room and pulled out a bottle of sparkling cider. We toasted Christopher House and the grant. Pastor gave thanks and said a prayer asking for God's strength and guidance as we prepared for this journey. It was a truly joyous moment—a moment of progress for Christopher House—a moment of clarity for myself.

* * *

Over the next few months, I registered for classes and walls came down as construction started in the backroom that would become a community health center. I spent a few mornings a week helping with whatever I could, carrying debris to the dumpsters outside, planning the hiring of staff, and the ribbon cutting.

I continued working at the after-school program until May when Allison and I were officially hired on and began our duties, hiring staff and preparing for the June 15 opening day. When the renovations were almost done, I invited Jeff and my sister for a tour. Jeff had been to the construction site several times as I coaxed him to put on his old jeans and running shoes and help me clear garbage and clean up. This was the first time for my sister. She had been busy working and finishing school. She was just about to graduate with her medical assistant certificate and was excited to see the facilities.

Afterward, we went out to dinner at a Thai restaurant down the block. Halfway through the meal, my sister looked up, "I have something you may want to know," she said over her bowl of wontons. "Mom's not doing too well. She's struggling without dad."

I shrugged and took a shallow breath. "What's going on exactly?"

"She's talking about selling the house and moving in with Aunt Sissy."

"Oh." I paused. "Do you think it's going to happen?"

"I think she wants to, but I'm not sure she has the strength or the ability to get it all done herself."

"You're probably right."

"I think Aunt Sissy and her family may help, but I was hoping you could help some too."

I reached out and put my hand on hers. "If you need me to help, I'll do what I can."

She smiled and we continued eating in silence.

"So." I looked at her a few minutes later. "I guess you'll be looking for a place to live then."

"Haven't thought that far ahead."

"Well, let me tell you—think about it—the other option isn't that pleasant. Trust me," I said, a hint of sarcasm in my voice.

She looked at me and squinted, not knowing if she was supposed to laugh or feel sorry for me. And then a tear bubbled up in her eye and trailed down her cheek.

"Hey, I didn't mean anything by that."

"I know. It's just hard for me to think about what happened to you."

"Don't worry—that's long gone. Everything's good now." I waited for a moment as trepidation rose in my throat. "I've got Jeff." I turned and looked at him and then back at my sister. "I've got the opportunity at Christopher House. I'm back in school. And we have a great apartment with our own little view of the sound." She looked at me trying to feel happy through her sad eyes. "You know I'll always be here for you," I said.

She sniffled.

I looked at Jeff and motioned my head toward my sister. He raised his eyebrows asking for silent clarification. And so I took my chance. "Jeff, we have two bedrooms."

"That we do," He said, smiling and nodding, letting me know he was in on the surprise.

"We don't use that second bedroom for much, do we?"

"Not much," Jeff said, shrugging and looking at me with a comforting smile.

"Well, what do we think about renting it out and making a bit of cash."

"I think that sounds like a good idea."

I looked at my sister, smile on her face, a full set of tears running down her cheeks. I paused for a moment and watched a tear drip off the end of her chin. "Well, how 'bout it, sis? You want to live with a couple love birds."

She nodded, her tears of sadness fully transformed to joy. "I think I could manage."

"It's settled then. Whenever you're ready, we'll move the extra boxes out and move you in."

* * *

Three weeks later, on a sunny Friday afternoon, ceremonial red ribbon stretched across the open door of Christopher House and a white sheet placed over a small sign displayed at the entrance, we gathered—Nadine, Pastor Jim, Kim, Hector, the other investors and contractors, a few city officials, and of course Jeff, my sister, Allison, and the nurses we hired in the last two weeks. And just as the ceremony began I noticed a familiar face finding a spot near the back of the crowd. I sent a personal message to Mr. Alinson two weeks ago, thanking him for his help and inviting him to the grand opening. I raised my hand and waived through the crowd. He held up a thumb in greeting.

We made a conscious decision not to displace the three tents that were a permanent part of the sidewalk decor in front of the entrance. They had become the unofficial welcome to those who entered and a continual reminder of our mission. We invited the owners of the tents and a few other people who lived in a nearby encampment for food and beverage and to be our inaugural patients in the clinic.

We cut the ribbon at two o'clock, pulled the sheet from the new Health and Welfare Clinic sign donated by the local arts consortium, and christened the clinic with a poem read by a local teacher. The sun was in the midst of its daily routine, floating amongst a few clear white clouds, sending down its rays of hope as it warmed the ground and the air around us. We celebrated with a tour of the facility and libations and welcomed our first few patients with health checkups and clean socks.

It was a few months of anticipation and sleepless nights coming to fruition, but it felt like a lifetime in the making. It was as if all my experiences led to that moment—the day I found out I was no longer enrolled in my classes—the day I knew I was no longer welcome in my parents' house—waking in the alley to the sound of newspapers hitting the pavement in front of the businesses near where I slept.

The sounds of the street were once my wake-up call and my life had become one long trudge through minutes, hours, and days—from tent to dumpster, from dumpster to soup kitchen, from soup kitchen to... My thoughts trailed off for a moment as voices around me caught my attention, but as I stood amongst the celebration I was once again drawn back to that short time in my life. I remembered walking along the pier aimlessly, hiding my face from the crowds of people filing in and out of shops and restaurants. I remembered finding myself sitting in the corner of an alleyway hiding behind heaps of garbage. My days were spent either in search of or hiding from—in search of my next meal or a warm jacket or a place to sleep—hiding from hunger, from sight, from a life I was ashamed to be living. But, I was no longer hiding—no longer living in the cracks and crevices of the city. I was no longer ashamed. I had made a complete one-hundred-and-eighty-degree transformation. It all came rushing at me—sights, sounds, emotions—and suddenly, I felt queasy. I turned in a circle looking for an open place to sit and catch my breath. I walked to the side of the room, sat on a folding chair, and closed my eyes.

A few moments later I felt a hand on my shoulder. I took a deep breath and looked up. "Are you okay," Jeff handed me a bottled water.

I took a sip. "Yeah, thanks." I took another sip. "It's just amazing." I looked around. "I'm trying to take it all in."

"It's amazing, alright. And you made all this possible."

"I may have had a hand in it, but it took everyone here. I mean, just think if my professor didn't give my paper to his friend. Every little thing counts. Every little thing makes a difference."

"You're right—it's a team effort."

"Hey guys, what you doing over here," my sister came bounding our way, light in her eyes.

"Just sitting back and watching everyone have a good time," I said, looking up at Jeff and then at my sister.

"Well, guess what I just did," she said, buzzing with energy.

"You met the man of your dreams?" I quipped.

"Nah, I've got you guys in my life already."

"Sure, we're quite the catch," Jeff said.

"So, what'd you just do?" I asked, seeing that she was about to boil over with excitement.

"I signed up to volunteer at the clinic."

"Sweet—you think you're up to it," I laughed.

"Yup. I graduate soon, so I thought I would put my training to good use and help out here for a while."

I stood up and hugged her and then took her hand and walked her and Jeff around the waiting room filled with buzzing emotion. I introduced them to Kim and Hector, to my professor, and to the two investors who I again thanked for their support. We drank some punch and snacked on crackers and cheese and then we helped clean up when the celebration was over.

That night we sat in our apartment, on a new couch we purchased when we moved in. I turned on the TV and we found a movie, ate popcorn, and laughed together as the narrative unfolded.

When I woke up Monday morning it felt like life had begun. The smell of coffee reminded me that Jeff was up early as usual, making breakfast and getting ready for work. I could hear the shower running in the bathroom and assumed my sister was eagerly preparing for her final week of school before she received her medical assistant certification.

I had a slight feeling of eagerness to start my week, as well. This was the first official day for our clinic, all the fanfare was in the rearview mirror and I was ready to jump right in. The doors would open at nine and I was charged with making sure everything was in its place.

When I arrived at the front door that morning I was the first one there. I reached into my pocket, listening to the jingle of my keys as I pulled them out and searched for the shiny gold one I was given as part of my new job. I slipped it into the keyhole and listened to the swish and click as I turned the key and unlocked the deadbolt. I reached for the worn brass handle, pressing the latch at the top with my thumb, slowly pulling it open. On this day, the day of new beginnings, I thought back to the first time I walked into that small waiting room containing a warn brown wooden desk with a monitor and phone sitting atop, three blue plastic chairs along the opposite wall, and a coffee table scattered with pamphlets and a bowl of condoms with a sign that read, *Take One and Be Safe.* I was once a person in distress. Today, I walked in as an employee, a person of change, a person who was there to serve. The waiting room was much the same, the blue plastic chairs had been replaced by two small couches and a small table on the far wall, the table where much of our planning for the clinic had been done, but it was still modest. It was still simple. It was still the place that gave me and many people the hope we needed to move forward.

I flicked on the lights, walked over, pulled the cord on the blinds, and watched the light flood the room. I walked to the back room and searched the fridge until I found a bag of six bagels. I walked out to the front of the building and greeted the three men huddled in their tents. I handed them the bagels and then went back in and found them three bottled waters. I made it a point to go out at least twice a week to say hi and bring them some food. Over time, I would find a new tent and a new inhabitant. I would introduce myself and make sure to learn their name. At one point, a sixteen-year-old girl moved in. Her name was Madeline. She ran away from home, escaping years of sexual abuse. She had nothing but a hooded sweatshirt, a small blanket, and a tent with a broken zipper. One day I arrived at work on a cold fall morning and found her shivering inside her tent with the flap wide open. I walked over to her, reached in, took her hand, and brought her into the clinic. When Allison arrived, she helped Madeline find some warm clothes and then we found her a bed in a women's shelter. A month later we found her a permanent home with a family member.

And that's how I wanted my life to be—serving—reaching out my hand and lifting people up. So it began on that first official day of the clinic.

Chapter Nineteen

As my life was being pulled in a number of wonderful directions—working with Allison from eight to one each weekday getting the program off the ground—spending afternoons and evenings taking classes and studying—I found a rare two-hour window of respite in an otherwise busy schedule, sitting quietly with Jeff in our apartment.

When I look back on that specific moment in time—days, weeks, even years later—I recall people asking me, "Was it romantic? Did he do something special? Did he get down on one knee?"

And I always reply, "He didn't do anything elaborate. He didn't take me to a far-off land or get down on one knee." I then pause—look at them and smile—and watch them wonder for a moment. I continue, "We sat there, on our little Juliet balcony, staring at our slice of the bay off in the distance, visible between the two adjacent apartments across the alleyway. He set his hand on mine softly as it lay on the metal bistro table that barely fit between us. 'This is all I need,' he said, eyes glued on the scene in front of us. We sat there for a moment and then he added sweetly, 'Will you marry me?' The wind blew softly as I gave myself a moment to control my trembling voice. 'Yes,' I replied gently. We turned toward each other without a word, a small tear welling up in the corner of his right eye. We turned back to the one-hundred-and-fifty-dollar-a-month view that takes us to blue waters and the far-off horizon, between the two adjacent buildings across the alleyway."

And with that, most, if not all, feel a little patter of sweetness roll around their stomach as their heart rate quickens the slightest bit. Many of them let out an audible moan or a whispered sigh, longing for that feeling, some maybe even relating to that feeling of love and comfort, but all moved to some degree or another by its simplicity.

Ten minutes later, the door opens inside the apartment and my sister enters. "I'm home." She calls. We turn, look through the opened sliding glass door behind us, and return her greeting. A few minutes more and the three of us gather in what to us felt like the most spacious kitchen you could imagine, even though we have to excuse our hands or our rear ends as we move, reach, stretch to find a mixing bowl or spoon or cup somewhere in the space we inhabit together—making a shared meal—a family meal.

Once my sister moved in not long after I offered the invitation over dinner and tears, we sat, many nights, at a table that fit us all, enjoying each other's company—enjoying our time together—enjoying the family we had created. We had what we needed to be happy. Jeff was right, "This is all we need."

* * *

We planned our wedding for the evening on a late spring day almost a year from the day I started working at Christopher House and going to night classes. It was both a wedding and an anniversary of sorts. We decided to forgo any big pre-wedding frivolities, in favor of reliving our first unofficial date. On the chosen day, Jeff woke up early, leaving me in bed with a cup of coffee, and borrowed his dad's motorcycle. An hour later he met me in front of our apartment building, bringing flashbacks of that awkward day he picked me up in front of the three-hundred-square-foot studio I lived in on my own and then eventually we lived in together.

We traveled the same route, down the same streets, across the same bridge, and to the same park. We walked the same paths at the park, passed the disc golf course, the softball field, and down to the beach. We even ate the same disappointing pizza before waiting in the same line to take the same ferry across the water. And then we continued to ride, my hands holding tightly around his waist, the bike purring beneath us until we arrived at the same little store on the side of the road.

We set our helmets on the bike and stood for a while, a déjà vu moment if there ever was one. Jeff ran his hands through his hair and looked around, a habit he had that was always endearing.

I took his hand and led him to the same bench we sat on in front of the store. We sat for a while, a soft breeze cooling the air. We looked at each other, then looked away and laughed.

"We need our root beers," I said as I stood up. "You up for one?" He smiled and nodded his head, his eyes catching the light and emitting a slight sparkle.

I emerged from the store with a cold can in each hand, just like before, sat next to him, and handed him his drink. The cans echoed as we popped them open and listened to the bubbles escape into the air. We sipped slowly, enjoying the sweetness—enjoying the suds as they tickled our noses, enjoying the memories and the nostalgia of a time that now means so much.

By the time our trip was over we had just enough time to shower, dress at the apartment, and make it to the ceremony. Tim offered the use of his parents' house when we invited him and Joey over for a housewarming and announced our engagement. His parents owned a place just outside town with a perfect backyard for about thirty people. And it was perfect— a few folding chairs, Tim and Joey standing up with Jeff, my sister and Nadine standing on my side, and Pastor Jim at the helm.

A short service led us to an outdoor barbecue and, as nine o'clock approached, Tim's dad lit their firepit and we sat around sharing stories as the flames danced in the waning light and illuminated our faces. And soon, night turned to morning, and the few friends who remained, stood, hugged, and vanished into the darkness.

* * *

I turned over and looked at my phone, sleep still blanketing my body. The blurry numbers read seven twenty-five. I turned back over and draped my left arm over Jeff's sleeping body, heavy breathing emitting from his side of the bed. I laid there for a moment and took a deep breath. Instead of a honeymoon, we decided to celebrate with brunch on the pier at one of our favorite restaurants, so I forced myself to get up, put on a pot of coffee, and jump in the shower. When I got out, Jeff was sitting on the couch, unkempt hair and heavy eyes, sipping his coffee. He forced a half-smile and grumbled a muffled good morning.

"You still want to go to brunch?" I asked.

"Once the eggs Benedict are in my stomach I'll feel better—

and maybe awake," he was trying to joke, but the lack of sleep had stolen his usual sarcasm and he looked like he was fighting the urge to crawl back under the covers.

We drank Mimosas in the bar as we waited for our table and our bodies and minds to find their equilibrium. After we filled our bellies and felt like we were awake enough to hold a decent conversation, we decided to walk along the pier and ride the great Ferris wheel overlooking the water. As our gondola made its way to the top of the arch, we had a clear view across the water and the ferries making their journey to the islands on the other side of the bay. The sun shone bright in the blue sky and waves crashed in the distance. Small boats made their way across the horizon. Gulls swooped to and fro, squawking as they swept to the ground and back into the air.

Back on the pier, we made the four-minute walk to the aquarium and watched the seals feeding in the window outside the entrance. We asked a young couple to take our picture in front of the fountain on the sidewalk. We spent some time roaming through shops, eating ice cream, and then made our way across the street, up the stairs, and walked through the fish market and maze of vendors. Before we headed home, we bought some fresh honey, some flowers, and a handmade card for my sister to celebrate her pending graduation.

* * *

The following weekend I found myself driving with Jeff and my sister to meet Aunt Sissy and help her pack my Mom's belongings into a truck. She had been out of the house for two weeks, but the house needed to be cleared out and cleaned so it could be put on the market.

When we arrived, Aunt Sissy was there with our cousin Phil. They were in the kitchen sorting through pots, pans, dishes, and all the other knickknacks that had gathered over decades.

"Sissy," my sister called as we walked in.

"Hey, guys, we're in the kitchen."

Sissy was a tough woman. She had been through a lot in her life. Her husband passed away after a long battle with cancer when her two children were just in elementary school. She had to raise them on her own and struggled to put food on the table for many years. But she was always there for her family, and our family too—babysitting, cooking Thanksgiving and Christmas meals—going on family vacations with us. She never seemed to run out of energy.

We met in the kitchen and gave each other big hugs. I hadn't seen Sissy or Phil in a half dozen years. We stood, talking, catching up, and then sharing ideas on what to do with all the old stuff in the house. We decided that if we found anything we wanted, we would pack it in our trunk. Whatever was left after we filled Mom's five boxes in the living room would be sold by an estate agency before the house went up for sale.

Apparently, my sister had explained my situation to Sissy because when I told her I wanted nothing to do with anything in the house she was totally on board with my feelings. She was always the cool Aunt. When we were young she and the cousins would come over and we would play with Phil and his sister Hillary in the backyard for hours and then she would bake pies or help us make homemade ice cream.

The house was eerily empty, even though most of my parents' stuff was still in the same place it was when I was in high school. All I wanted to do was pack the boxes and leave, but two hours later we were sitting on the front porch reminiscing about our escapades in the backyard and the summer trips our families took together almost twenty years ago. Surprisingly, it ended up being rather cathartic, spending time with my favorite Aunt and then finally putting this old life to rest. I felt it was one more thing I had packed away and put in the rearview mirror.

Before we left I took one last trek around the house, filing the memories away in the deep recesses of my mind. I knew I didn't want to think about them again in the near future, but I figured I might want access to them at some point. We walked outside together and looked at the fort we built the summer after I graduated fifth grade. We spent many hours playing pirates or superheroes, saving the galaxy, and flying off to far-off lands. It felt nice to remember the good times when everything surrounding the house and my parents over the past handful of years felt so awful.

I gave Aunt Sissy a big hug and thanked her for the help. She wished us well and we left—on our way back to the life we had built on our own—on our way back to the life that was no longer part of the old house—no longer part of the parents and the memories that used to inhabit the now vacant house—the house that felt a lifetime away.

Chapter Twenty

Time went by quickly. Days were jam-packed with activity—part-time at the clinic and full-time in night school filled every waking hour. Days went by in a flash. Weeks went by like days. And soon it was almost Thanksgiving and I was officially certified as a clinical psychologist. Allison had already been showing me how to handle paperwork and documentation, but now I was ready to start seeing my own clients.

I started by meeting with one client in the morning and one in the afternoon. This gave me a chance to ease into the process. Since I had been working at the clinic for six months and could personally relate to many of my clients' situations, I was able to move quickly into three, four, and then, right before the new year, I added a fifth—however, the fifth was not by choice.

I woke up early on December 30 and walked to the window of my bedroom. A few soft flakes floated from the light gray skies above—a blustery wind disturbed their trajectory and blew them haphazardly about. Jeff was gone to an early meeting. My sister was tucked in bed, no work today, but she was scheduled to volunteer at the clinic around noon.

I got ready for the day, wrapped a scarf around my neck, zipped my winter jacket up to my chin, and set out. When I arrived at work, I checked on a new set of tent campers and then got each a thick blanket and a cup of hot coffee. The day moved on, as usual, filled with clients in the medical clinic, and new faces in the counseling center. After lunch, I was sitting at a table on the far side of the room pecking away at my laptop when my sister came up, put her hands on the table, and quietly told me there was a young woman who was asking for me. I looked over and did not recognize her from behind.

"She said you've helped her before." My sister clarified when she saw the confusion on my face.

"Yeah, okay. Tell her I'll be right there." I closed my computer and gathered my stuff. I walked over to the young woman and squatted down a few feet away from her. She was sitting with a blanket wrapped around her shoulders, elbows on her knees, and a cup of hot chocolate in trembling hands. She was staring down at her dirty white shoes, scraggly brown hair hanging in front of her face.

"Hello," I said softly.

She tilted her head slightly and peeked through the hair that camouflaged her identity. "Hi," she replied, her voice barely audible.

I turned my head sideways, trying to get a view of the person behind the hair. "How can I help you?"

She didn't answer right off. But then, with a shaky voice, "I don't know—I'm not sure."

"You said I helped you before."

"Yes—a while ago."

"Okay—I can't see your face behind your hair," I said slowly. "Do you mind helping me out?"

She looked up and brushed her hair away from her face. Revealing a gaunt, yet familiar image. "Oh, Madeline. I remember you." I turned and looked to see if the office was free. "Do you want to go into the office? We can talk privately."

"Okay," she whispered, still looking down at her dingy shoes.

"Do you mind if I ask Allison to join us?" I looked at her with a smile. "She's the other counselor who helped you last time."

"Sure," a meek voice replied.

I led her to the office and had her sit in one of the two soft armchairs in front of the desk. "Hold on. I'll be right back." I walked out to the admin counter where my sister was talking to one of the nurses. "Excuse me, would one of you find some clean clothes for Madeline—the young woman in my office?" I turned and looked back at Madeline. She was sitting, huddled in an almost fetal position. "She's going to need a hot shower and a meal, too."

"Yeah, I'll help with that," my sister said.

"And when she's ready, I'll help her with a shower," the nurse added.

"Thanks—and would one of you have Allison meet me in our office?"

"I'll find Allison," the nurse replied.

I walked back into the office and sat behind the desk, making sure to keep the door open so Madalin would feel comfortable. "So, how long has it been since we saw each other last? It's got to be at least six months."

"Uh-huh," a slight whispered reply.

I sat for a minute, letting her get comfortable with me in the room. "Do you mind if I ask you a few questions to see how I can help you?"

"Yeah, sure." She stole a quick look at me through her greasy hair.

"I just want you to know, the questions I ask are just to see what I can do for you. If you feel uncomfortable answering anything, you don't have to."

She sat quietly—looking down at the floor.

"So, first off, are you sick or hurt in any way?"

"No—not really," her voice trailed off.

"What do you mean by, not really?"

"I'm not sick. At least, I don't think I am."

"How are you feeling physically?"

She took a shallow breath and shrugged. "A bit weak."

"Do you remember the last time you ate?"

"Yesterday—sometime in the morning."

"Do you remember what you had to eat?"

"I went to a friend's house when her parents were at work and had some eggs."

My sister knocked on the door. She had a folded pile of clothes in her hands. I motioned to the chair next to Madeline. She set them down, smiled at Madeline who did not look up, and then quietly walked out.

"When we're done talking, you can take a shower and put on some clean clothes if you'd like." Just then, a soft knock and Allison appeared in the doorway. I stood up. "Madeline, do you remember Allison? She was here last time you came in." Madeline looked up and nodded. I looked at Allison. "Madeline and I are just having a little conversation. She was here about six months ago. We helped her find a place to stay with relatives."

"Yes, I remember," Allison said with a motherly air. She always had a way of bringing a sense of comfort into the room and this time was no different. I could see Madeline's shoulders relax immediately and she sat a little taller in her chair. The cadence of Allison's voice, the sweetness in her demeanor, seemed to help everyone feel safe. I noticed this for the first time just three days after we started working together. Two young gang members were nose to nose in the waiting room, posed for more than a simple confrontation. Allison entered, and five minutes later, the two young men were sitting across from each other on the couches in the middle of the room, not totally calm, but separated and breathing with a sense of regularity.

"Do you want to join us?" I smiled at her and gestured toward the seat with the clean clothes.

"Sure—if it's okay with Madeline."

Madeline nodded.

We continued talking for another ten minutes. She started to relax. She told us she ran away from her Aunt's house about two weeks ago. The last week was spent hiding in the storage shed behind a friend's house.

"So, why'd you leave your Aunt's house," I asked.

"Umm—well—she was forcing me to talk with my dad."

"Okay." I jotted down a few notes. "Was that over the phone or in person?"

"One day I came home from school and they were in the kitchen talking. I heard his voice and ran up to my room."

"Did she ask you if you wanted to talk with him?"

"Not really. I guess my dad called her after I was there for a few weeks and he wanted to see me, but I said no."

"What did she say when you told her no?"

"She didn't say much. She just said I should talk things over with him because he was sorry."

"Did she say what he was sorry for?"

"No."

"Does she know what he was doing to you?"

"I think so, but I don't think she fully believed me."

"And then how long after this conversation did you find him

at your house."

"Maybe a week or two."

"That must have been a few months ago, right?"

"The first time. But he came over maybe three times. And I had to get out of there."

"If you were to go back to your Aunt's house, would you feel safe?"

"No—I mean, I don't think she would do anything, but I also don't think she would stop my dad from doing anything."

"Alright—we won't make you go back there." We sat for a few minutes while I took notes. "Okay, can you excuse Allison and me for a minute? I want to get you something to eat."

"Sure."

Allison and I walked out of the office. "Can you make sure she gets some food and a shower? I want to call the Domestic Abuse Hotline."

"Yeah. What are you thinking?"

"I'm not sure if we have grounds to keep her here, especially since the only beds we have are technically for men, so I want to find out our options."

"Alright. Sounds like you know what you're doing. I'll make sure she gets fed and cleaned up."

I made the phone call and found out there wasn't much we could do except turn her father in on child abuse charges. In the meantime, she would probably have to go back to her Aunt's house unless there was another family member or guardian who was willing to take her in. I asked how long she was able to stay at Christopher House, but that was not a long-term option since it was a men's shelter—and they also told me since she was almost seventeen, the charges against her father would probably still be pending when she turned eighteen. I asked them about using Christopher House as sanctuary since church services were held there once a week and thus it was technically a place of worship. Another roadblock was thrown up, as they told me that having a religious service at a facility does not make the facility a place of worship. By the time the phone call was done, I didn't have any more answers than before I called—but, what I did have was resolve. I was pissed. I hung up the phone and stormed outside. It was their job to help keep her safe, but all they had were excuses and dead ends.

I walked around the block, trying to keep my cool. I had never felt this angry before and by the time I walked back in the front door, I had made a decision. I would do whatever it takes to keep Madeline safe. Allison suggested I consult with Pastor and Nadine. "They have been working with this type of thing for years and may have some good ideas," she said. Pastor Jim told me to set a bed up for her in the counselor's office, that way she could have privacy and stay safe. Then, we needed to find a few female staff members willing to split shifts and stay with her overnight until we could figure out the next step.

We asked for volunteers willing to spend the night and quickly my sister, Allison, and one of the nurses stepped up. They each took a one-night shift and we hoped that would give us enough time to find a more permanent solution. Two days later, after a follow-up call, a representative of the county's domestic abuse center made a surprise visit to check on the situation. They urged us to take her back to her Aunt's house.

"How do you even know her Aunt wants her back?" I said with an unfiltered note of irritation.

"We're going to follow up on the situation, but you need to prepare her for that possibility."

"I'm not going to do that. I'm not going to let her be put back into that situation."

"You may have no choice."

"I'm going to find another option," I said, trying to control my anger.

"Well, we are going to contact her Aunt. In the meantime, the right thing to do would be to prepare her to go."

The representative left and it was all I could do not to kick him in the ass as he walked out the door. I gathered Allison, Pastor, and Nadine and explained to them what the domestic violence representative told me.

"That's common," Pastor said. "They have a rule book they have to follow. If she was younger, they would make a bigger effort to make sure she was safe. Since she's almost an adult, they're just waiting for time to pass so she can live on her own."

"What about your church?" I asked.

"My church?"

"It's a place of worship—and doesn't it have a Pastor's quarters."

"Ahh, it does," he said, perking up a bit.

"Can we move her there while we find her a permanent place?"

"Yeah—we should be able to do that. Good idea."

A week later, the representative from the domestic abuse center called to check up on her. "I'm calling to let you know Madeline's Aunt would like her to move back in."

"That's not an option," I replied.

"What do you mean, that's not an option?"

"She's already somewhere safe."

"Is she still at Christopher House?"

"No. She has a safe place to live."

"We'd like to have her contact information so we can check

up on her."

"I'm afraid that's not possible. She's claiming asylum," I explained as I stood, an immovable force, ready to do whatever it took to make sure she was safe.

And that's where it stood. We held off the authorities, both from the state and the county, long enough to find her a place to live, at least until she turned eighteen and graduated from high school. I ended up calling Kim and Hector and, again, they came to the rescue. They found a friend who was a certified foster parent willing to take care of her for the next sixteen months, just enough time to get her through the remainder of her junior and senior years.

A little over a year later I was sorting through the mail at work when I came across an envelope with my name on it. It was a graduation announcement from Madeline. She wrote: *To my saviors at Christopher House. Thank you for everything you did for me. I will be graduating in June and will be attending the local technical college. Frank and Janine said I can continue to live with them while I get my veterinary assistant certification. I've always loved animals and I will always love you guys.*

I shared the card with Allison, Nadine, Pastor, and all the nurses. We shed a few tears and said a prayer. When I got home I showed the card to Jeff and my sister and then the three of us squeezed onto our Juliet balcony staring at our slice of the bay off in the distance, visible between the two adjacent apartments across the alleyway. We shared little stories about our days and then Jeff set his hand on mine softly as it lay on the metal bistro table that barely fit between us. We sat there for a moment and then my sister added sweetly, "This is all I need." We turned toward each other without a word, a small tear welling up in the corner of her right eye. I smiled at her and then at Jeff and then we turned back to the one-hundred-and-fifty-dollar-a-month view that takes us to blue waters and the far-off horizon, between the two adjacent buildings across the alleyway.

Later we shared a communal meal, made in our spacious kitchen, the one we had to excuse our hands or our rear ends as we moved, reached, stretched to find a mixing bowl or spoon or cup somewhere in the space we inhabited together. But, it was our kitchen. It was our life. And this was our family. We ate and we talked. We ate and we laughed as we did many nights.

And it was at that moment I finally realized, the world no longer hovered around me. I was no longer a bystander while the happenings of the world went on without me. I was now a part of the world. I was a servant. I was a change-maker. And that is what I was called upon this earth to be.

Also by Adam C. France

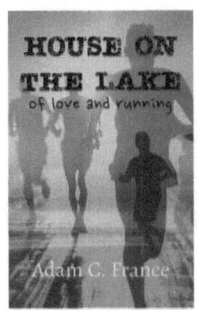

House on the Lake: of love and running
Available Now: Set against the backdrop of a budding romance and societal challenges, the story follows the protagonist as he discovers his passion for running while pursuing a love that defies racial boundaries.

Fighting For Loose Change
Winter 2024 release: The story takes you from the field behind the apartments to a state title to the dark underbelly of the fight world, exploring the emotional entanglement and self-discovery of a character with an addictive personality as he learns to deal with a trait that afflicts many.

www.ingramcontent.com/pod-product-compliance
Lightning Source LLC
Chambersburg PA
CBHW050837180626
46814CB00007B/2509